The Road to Ballyshannon

The Road to Ballyshannon

DAVID MARTIN

215296

St. Martin's Press
New York

Library of Congress Cataloging in Publication Data

Martin, David, 1937-
    The road to Ballyshannon.

    1. Ireland—History—1625-1649—Fiction.   I. Title.
PR6069.T497R6   1983   823'.914   83-9720
ISBN 0-312-68514-9

First published in 1981 in Great Britain by Martin Secker & Warburg Limited.

First U.S. Edition

10 9 8 7 6 5 4 3 2 1

for
Vincent Mahon
our thoughts on
Inis Saimer
and
Lynda
who took us there

Consider the herds that are feeding yonder: they know not the meaning of yesterday or today: . . . Man cannot see them without regret, for even in the pride of his humanity he looks enviously on the beast's happiness. He wishes simply to live without satiety or pain, like the beast; yet it is all in vain, for he will not change places with it. He may ask the beast—'Why do you look at me and not speak to me of your happiness?' The beast wants to answer—'Because I always forget what I wished to say'; but he forgets this answer, too, and is silent: and the man is left to wonder.

He wonders also about himself – that he cannot learn to forget, but hangs on the past: however far or fast he runs, that chain runs with him.

The Use and Abuse of History
Friedrich Nietzsche

Though no one escaped from the prison-ship *Argenta*, which was moored in Larne Lough from 1920 until 1924, escapes have been made from such prison-ships both before and since, the last being from the *Maidstone*, anchored in Belfast Lough, in 1972. But though I have used the *Argenta*, as I have certain command structures of forces engaged in hostilities during the civil war period, the characters in this book are purely fictitious and bear no resemblance to any person or persons living or dead.

D.M.   Belfast, 1980.

The author wishes to acknowledge the assistance of the Arts Council of Northern Ireland in the writing of this novel.

The Road to Ballyshannon

One

It came in with the incoming tide. In the narrow channel where the mainland tapered into the granite conical-topped tower and stood as though a sentinel facing the spur of the peninsula, the triangular shape of the dorsal fin could be momentarily seen in the cloudy light of a winter afternoon. Again it appeared, the fine razor edge creating a glint of white foam on the dull waters, and vanished.

They had been anticipating its appearance. Over half the time allotted to the exercise period had now passed, during which the two figures who kept close to the stern of the ship had anxiously traced every wave and ripple of the lough surface, had watched the landmass on either side almost imperceptibly alter as the vessel was buoyed up with a clinking and creaking of chains and wires. As it appeared for the third time, a now motionless dark shape, made practically invisible by the quickly darkening sky, the younger of the two men grasped his companion's wrist.

'Look! There.'

'Easy, easy,' whispered the older, releasing himself from the grip of the other. 'Remember. If it can get through the wire just so, then so can we. Don't forget that.'

They were an incongruous pair, the boy's fresh unmarked face flushed by the cold sea wind making him seem much less than his nineteen years; the man's seamed, scarred, with narrow black eyes turned inwards as though constantly searching

9

the depths of himself and oblivious to anything outside, yet eyes which were always first to observe the arrival of the dolphin as it approached the prison-ship, and its departure.

They had been watching it for three weeks now. The man had noticed it first, a black upturned vee caught in the rays of a reddish winter sun. Silently he pointed it out to the boy, and both had watched as it circled the ship, vanishing at regular intervals. The last time it appeared it was directly underneath them and indistinctly they could see the massive powerful back and slowly moving tail. Then it was gone.

For three weeks it had come without fail. In the first few days it had simply become an object of curiosity, this rare phenomenon of a fully grown dolphin leaving the trackless depths of the sea to penetrate the narrow mouth of Larne Lough: for the man, a beast of the ocean never seen before in all his forty-four years and which bore no resemblance whatsoever to the beasts of the land he knew intimately; for the boy, a sensuous curving shape stirring the imagination and bringing to mind other times he had seen one. Mostly it had been in foreign waters, except for that one moonlit night towards Scotland when, with others, he had been following the herring and there, between the dark jutting mass of Ailsa Craig and the winking beaming eye of Port Patrick throwing slivers of light across the surface of the Moyle, it rose and fell in perfect rhythm but a few yards for'ard of the bow, a thing of wonder, beauty, its back glistening with stars like the stars in the sky as it swam and plunged between the craggy face of Paddy's Milestone and the sweeping eye of Paddy's Lighthouse, plunging among the stars. To his mind had come fragments of sailors' tales centuries old, tales of the dolphin, man's friend of the sea, an omen of good fortune from unimaginable regions. And that night had seen many herring brought inboard, the boat so heavy with a seething mass of bright silver that they risked swamping.

Inarticulately he had tried to tell his companion what the dolphin was, but the man's eyes, though fixed on him, showed no comprehension. His mind was locked, fixed on the hard flinty earth which had grudgingly sustained him in his labour, which had made the tough sturdy breed of cow and sheep fight it in order to wrest from it their food. Above his head the mountains rose always, hard, scarred, inscrutable, like his own face and body, like his own mind. The beasts common to his knowledge he treated as the hard mountain land he worked treated him, leaving them alone when they left him alone, pursuing them coldly, painstakingly, almost indifferently, in a winter so bitter that it would drive a big dog fox to attack a cow even within sight of the man, or would send a badger rooting among the fowl and, if trapped, make it erupt in a blazing vicious fury that could see the man's leg severed from his body. These beasts he knew.

'She's under us,' the man said, again in a whisper.

The feminine pronoun was apt. For both, it was a goddess which rose up beneath them. For the man, a mysterious visitation from something whose home was an element totally unknown, for the boy an undulating sensuous shape exciting mind and flesh in an image of the richness of bright silver.

Surreptitiously the boy slipped the meagre scraps of vegetable and meat between the thick wire mesh strung from the ship's rail to the superstructure, pieces carefully, reverently put to one side of the tin plate and then hidden in his pocket. Intently he listened, mind concentrating on their unseen fall, hearing the almost indistinct plopping sound as they hit the surface. He didn't know whether it accepted his offerings. But he liked to think that that was why it always returned. For the food. For his food.

For the man, it was sufficient that it came.

After the first few days it became the centre of their lives. Below decks, in the compartment they shared with many others, the man had stretched out his lengthy frame on the makeshift bunk, brooding. When they had been brought on board the prison-ship, it had not been long before his mind was fashioning a plan of escape. It was all there, except the last piece. Even when they managed to get over the side, they would still be trapped because of the network of wires fixed several feet down from the ship's sides and stretching far below the surface of the water. Caught, they would drown within minutes in the freezing lough. Day and night he brooded, seeing no way that they could get beyond it. Then the dolphin came, and he watched it with an idle curiosity, only to smile at his own stupidity a few days later. When the dark shape appeared beneath them without sending any of the wires jangling and so arousing the alarm of their captors, that meant there was a way in and a way out. When the time came they would be waiting for it, and would follow it out to freedom. To freedom, and to fight again.

'What happens if somebody else sees it?'

That was the boy's fear, and his own fear. 'They haven't yet. And it'll soon be the day,' the man whispered, walking away from his companion towards midships as the bell clanged to signal that the exercise period had ended. Yes, the day would have to be soon. Very soon.

The boy paused, taking from this last moment all he could, a spasm of fear making him catch his breath as he thought of returning to be locked up in the cages and decks below. Sometimes he would dream of the ship being sunk by one of the winter gales which sent heavy seas bursting into the narrow lough from the seething waters of the Moyle. He could see himself floating, dead, a limp body slowly bumping against the bars and bulkheads with the motion of the tide. Like the others. A whole fearful company of them floating around hitting one another as though wrestling, embracing, dancing. He'd seen drowned men before. One in particular stuck in his mind. The figure was caught in an anchor chain, lolling almost in a sitting position, swaying to and fro, to all intents resting in a rocking-chair. But it was the head which terrified him, the head with the mouth seemingly opening and closing as though the man was talking to him. Talking even while dead.

And sometimes he would dream of being free. Of leaving the thatched cottage in Glenarm where he was born to look up at the glens falling back inland in purples and greens and browns against a patchwork sky, an impenetrable spaciousness that made him feel dwarfed, awed. Of leaving the lodging house in

Larne where he would stay for a few days when his boat returned, not quite sure of what he was doing or where he was going, though the new suit and tie and shirt and seaman's raincoat casually unbelted gave the impression of rakish confidence, of standing at the bar listening to the talk and laughter of the men, seamen like himself from all quarters and of all colours, railwaymen, dockers, trying to understand this new world opening before him. Of spinning on the dance floor with the sweet aroma of perfume making him feel sick and dizzy, of seeing her breasts with the single dark hair from the left nipple pale in the bright summer night that flooded him with a savage excitement that was new but which he had somehow always known. Her breasts. The day she had waded in the stream with her frock tucked into her knickers, her slender tapering thighs arrogantly mocking his own hard angry timidity by their very proximity. That was an earlier image, when he was thirteen and just before he had gone to sea. As yet she had no singular form. She was all women. Even the prostitute who had taken him home one night and he, drunk, afraid, had lain in sweating hopelessness as the girl had vainly tried to rouse him. That was she also.

Except for one other. A Chinese girl in the East who, even in his youth, was already a dim memory. But he remembered the song. Love is kind. Love is kind to the least of men.

But the dream had always vanished, whether a dream of fear or joy, melting into the sight of bulkheads and bars. It was then he would think of his arrest when trying to smuggle guns. Guns for the Republican cause. And he would think also of his interrogation in the police cell and then crossing the lough in a rowing boat to the ship that was nothing but a huge cage floating on the water. A political prisoner.

'Why aren't you below?'

The voice was harsh but the hand which gripped his shoulder, though firm, wasn't brutal. He turned to face the guard, one of the few whose deeds belied their voice and tone.

'I'm going.'

'Jump to it, then.' The guard released his grip and said softly,

'Don't worry. You won't be in this cage all your life.'

The boy looked fleetingly into the other's eyes. The smile of comfort wasn't on the guard's face, but rather lay in the way he said what he said. He took another quick glance at the Island-magee side of the lough towards the small harbour at Millbay. Very dimly, a light glowed. Inside that light would be the talk and laughter and warmth of a small spirit-grocer. He shivered, almost feeling the glass of hot amber liquid of whisky and cloves being pushed into his hand.

The hand on his back was rougher this time. 'You were told to get going!'

He took another quick look towards the dark land-mass which squeezed the lough in from either side, but could see nothing. Then there was only bulkheads, bars.

He never dreamed about the dolphin. But perhaps that was because it was so largely a part of his wakened mind.

The man watched the boy hurriedly descend the ladder, the guard at his heels. Quickly the cage door was opened, then locked behind him. He stood for a moment blinking his eyes in the harsh glare of electric light, then crossed to a corner and stretched himself out on a bunk of flimsy wooden boards and sacking. Inside the cage, man and boy hardly acknowledged one another. That was his wish, the man's. His command. They'd find themselves close enough very soon. Perhaps too close. When they escaped. As soon as he'd started to think of a plan of escape, he'd also been trying to decide upon a companion. While the others prowled around the cage, talking, arguing, engaging in a bitter slanging match, he lolled somnolently against a bulkhead, watching through partly closed eyelids. He was first for food, pushing the gelatinous substance into his mouth without apparent haste, yet was first to finish. From a corner he again watched his fellow prisoners as they devoured the sodden lumps, cursing, complaining, joking, though with a bitter edge to their words. Some, mostly newcomers, the pangs in their bellies not yet sufficiently savage to make the offering palatable, pushed or kicked the food away with grunts. Those who weren't newcomers and who refused the food had, he decided, already given up. Theirs was hopelessness. And later, standing on deck during the exercise period, carefully scrutinising the winter landscape folding back in mizzle and gloom, he thought of the raw bloody flesh of rabbit or pigeon. They would refuse that too. They weren't survivors.

Others he counted out for a variety of reasons. Physical ailments were one thing. Once they had made good their escape, the trek to Ballyshannon would be arduous. Roughly one hundred miles as the crow flies. Add on half of that again for their journey. Travelling at around twenty-five to thirty miles a night, it would take them six or seven days. But it was the middle of winter. Good in one way, as they'd melt into the gloom of the long hours of darkness, into the almost constant mist and mizzle of the hills and valleys which made the light even heavier and filled a man's sight with wraiths, that is, unless they were conditions he knew intimately. Which was doubtful where the soldiers were concerned. They'd be mostly city men or foreigners. English. Not so the police. They would know the terrain almost as well as he did himself. Almost, but not quite. Yet it was bad in another way because it would make the going slow with the land soft, slippery, boggy, treacherous. Yes, they'd be hunted. That they could be certain of. East to west, travelling slightly south. Add on another two to six days for the going and the unforeseen. Ten to fourteen days, roughly. Across Antrim and along the northern shore of Lough Neagh through Tyrone and Fermanagh to the tip of Lower Lough Erne at Pettigo. Pettigo, which the British army shelled in the summer, disputing the land tracts of partition, of division. A few miles, then, to Ballyshannon in Donegal and to freedom, to Donegal Bay and the broad sweep of the Atlantic ocean.

And to fight. The civil war was all around, eddying outwards the summer before in the sound of field guns shelling the Four Courts in Dublin, disseminating even greater distrust and savagery, spilling over the hastily demarcated borders of the breakaway six counties of the north-east. Ireland divided. But was it escape to the Free State? Or to the Republic?

15

But first there were the freezing waters of Larne Lough and following the dolphin through the wires.

Others he discounted also. Those who found solace in the foul mixture brewed from slops that found its way into the cages and had a potency more of poison than of alcohol, unleashing savage quarrels and garrulous sentimentality alike. Those who surreptitiously sought the guards' favours. Those so unstable or witless that they showed their nature and risked being broken in solitary confinement. And there were the few like himself so withdrawn that it inhibited correct judgement of their character.

The guards had put them into separate cages, sifting the hundreds of prisoners into groups of pro-Treatyites and anti-Treatyites. Over the weeks and months, a running commentary was set up on the progress of the civil war, the guards sardonically embroidering each piece of information so that few could tell whether it was fact or fiction. Only the newcomers could do that, and soon they too became ensnared in a web of rumour and fancy.

To the guards he was a model prisoner, if such a term could be applied, given the conditions of captivity. Aloof, alone, he simply accepted circumstances and companions through sleepy eyes with a resigned stoicism. For the other prisoners he was a man apart, wanting nothing and giving nothing, a man from the mountains whose leonine energies could be sensed in the long, slightly hunched frame and hawkish face and loping gait, a man whose Republicanism was as deep as the origins of Republicanism itself.

He was from Tyrone, farming a small-holding at the foot of the Sperrin mountains just as his fathers had done. Centuries before, his people had been driven from the rich pasture lands of mid-Ulster by successive flurries of English and Scots settlers who stubbornly worked the soil, steeping it with the blood of the indigenous population, as with their own. He had heard those stories from childhood, sitting among the barren crags, looking across the opulent plains and valleys. In Ulster it was all like that. His people pushed to the fringes of existence. The lamentations over a silent land of hundreds of years before and still softly sung were part of his being. Songs of exile. Of a nobility dead. A nobility to return yet who never would return now. A melancholia that was sweet and bitter and persuasive.

Even in the cities it was like that, though he didn't know much of the cities, his people inhabiting the fringes, huddling in the poorer stretches. Derry. He'd been several times to Derry, to Belfast only a few. In the cities the buildings overpowered him, closed him in and squeezed him between them so that he could hardly breathe. Used to sheer rock though he was, the sheer sides of the taller buildings made him feel dizzy, just as the noise clogged his ears in a cacophonous medley which made him long for the clear sharp bark of a fox or the throated sound of a hawk snatching its prey. The people too were foreign, as though the narrow streets and sooty shed-like houses had branded them with their own mean appearance. The mountains had space, air.

It was in Derry he had been picked up, soon after the Republican army had split in two over the Treaty. He had gone to Derry, to Donegal too, to listen to the impassioned speeches for and against. The aftermath of the war of independence against England hadn't brought the hoped-for joy of victory. Abroad in the land was a spirit of febrile exhaustion, becoming rancid and bitter over a Treaty which many claimed was nothing more than the old state of servitude under a new name, a Treaty in which a minority could force the partition of the country at will, while backed by the power of England and its empire. Among his comrades-at-arms he listened to the protesting voices, to the voices of assent, knowing instinctively that his own choice was to keep the Republican spirit pure and inviolable and that many of the faces of old comrades now at his side would soon become the faces of his enemies.

The Division of which he was a member had taken the same choice. Those willing to accept the Treaty had quietly collected their arms and disappeared south, joining up elsewhere with a Division prepared to support the new Provisional Government. All over the country it was the same, the army becoming two

17

armies. Some simply went to ground, refusing to take part in the civil war about to be unleashed.

He was on his mountain farm when news came of the Republican stand in the Four Courts in Dublin. Summoned to Derry, he'd quickly gone, leaving wife and children to manage. But the enemy in the north was still the British army and the armed police, the newly formed RUC determined to secure the border and still all opposition within it. He didn't carry a gun, used to past experiences of sudden searches. Crossing the city he was stopped twice and then released, a hill farmer with a bulky sack on his shoulder, wares brought to the city markets to sell.

In a small house in the back streets of the city the talk had been confused. Despite the civil war, they were to continue as before. Commanders from the south and west came bringing orders. In the north there would be no split. The war was still against the British and would continue. But, the faces around him asked, how could they be really effective with the old unity gone? How could they fight when a civil war was taking place to determine what they were actually fighting for? Confusion, dissension, the old purpose weakened. He sensed it among them, and understood. In the south the leaders had already committed a kind of betrayal by asking for an impossibility. The guns were there, the logic, but the spirit was rapidly evaporating. While the new state now coming into being in the south exhausted itself further, those in the north could only skirmish ineffectually on the sidelines while the British forces and government of this new northern state contemptuously increased their strength at will. Even though the civil war swept past them, they were the ones who were truly caught. But if in all this he saw the shape of the future, he gave no sign.

And contemptuous also was his capture. Whistles sounded to announce that the area had been sealed off, announcing also that the long suspected emergency powers and dawn raids in Republican areas had now been brought into operation. The few who drew guns were dealt with, overwhelmed by weight of numbers. He had acted quickly, hastily slithering over several yard walls to step out of the back door of a corner house into a narrow stinking entry. Emerging from the entry into the evening sunlight, the sack again on his shoulder, he'd been searched again. But this time the ruse didn't work. During the week spent in the police cells they didn't tell him if they knew who he was: a Brigade Commandant of the 2nd Northern Division, but it was mentioned when he was transferred to the *Argenta*. He neither confirmed nor denied.

'When?'

They were bedding down, most of the prisoners pulling blankets and fragments of clothing tightly around themselves against the damp air which seeped through the cages of the ship from every angle and chilled a man's body the way frost could never do. It stiffened the bones and caught the chest in a cold clammy band. The boy's foot had caught his as the former stumbled over the already recumbent forms towards a corner, the single word sent spinning towards him.

'Soon.'

He was one of the last to lie down, as always, tugging a single blanket casually across his lengthy form as though spurning even meagre comfort. He slept lightly, his ears attuned to the rhythmic wash of the water against the ship's sides, a pattern which, if disturbed, would immediately arouse his senses. Yet when he awoke he was refreshed. It was a necessity, this kind of sleep, and something he had learned in the mountains. But this time when he became fully conscious he recalled that some part of his sleep had been disturbed, though not from outside. He had dreamed of Collins. Of Childers too. The Englishman.

It was three days before they saw the dolphin again. It lay motionless beneath them in the black water, almost touching the ship. He could sense the boy's excitement as the latter pressed his face against the wire netting to obtain a better view. The bright cold day etched the lines of the hills sharply across the sky. It would be good to be among the hills again. Patiently he anticipated the escape. It would be during the late afternoon exercise period when dusk was falling rapidly. Towards the stern was a hatch, rarely used, which led to the engine room.

There they would hide. The boy would fuse part of the lighting system which bathed the deck in a harsh glare, then they'd make their way to the side of the ship looking towards the mainland. Starboard, the boy had said. Once there they would quickly undo the bolts which secured the wire netting, bolts which he'd been working on for months, three in number, sufficient to allow them to slip through and drop as quietly as possible into the water. It would be better if the weather were bad so that the splash wouldn't be heard, even though the short swim could then prove difficult. The boy had warned him of the currents. Better still if there were another vessel nearby to distract the guards' attention. The dredger perhaps, which was constantly at work in the lough. He knew that the guards were casual about counting prisoners, as few believed that escape was possible.

Furtively he tested the bolts again as he walked. They were loose and turned instantly on his touch. That had been the hardest part. One had already been loose, and that had given him the idea. He'd waited for a week to see if the guards would notice it too. But no. Then he went to work on the other two, greasing them with blobs of fat from the previous evening's meal, knotting around them a thick piece of wire he'd procured from down the engine hatch, day after day keeping his seamed torn fingers from the sight of others. Eventually they yielded to his intense methodical determination and he greased them thoroughly and spun them tight again, to all intents secured fast to any but the most diligent eye.

The sound of a carol came over the clear calm air. Their trek would be during Christmas. And it would be the New Year before they reached Donegal. A good time, he thought, as there'd probably be a lull in activities and thus less chance of their being captured again. Yet as he listened to the wavering notes some deeper instinct moved within him, and he wondered if it were an omen.

When?

That one word was constantly on his mind. He went to sleep

with it, wakened with it. As the days slowly passed he sometimes felt as though the word was branded on his forehead, a
sure sign to alert the guards. The man hadn't told him yet how
they were going to do it. He wondered about that, at moments
believing that it was all just idle daydreaming, at others knowing that the man wouldn't tell him too soon in case he was
betrayed. He had the look of someone who wouldn't trust
anyone very much, with those partly closed eyes set back into
his head that never seemed to see anything yet which you knew
were watching you. They made him feel nervous.

The thought of the escape itself also made him feel nervous.
Even if they managed to reach the shore successfully, there was
the long hike across country to Donegal with the army and
police alerted. And if the talk of the guards was to be believed,
the whole of the north was like one huge army camp. Every
week, they said, saw more troops come in as the civil war in the
south worsened.

They wouldn't hole up in the vicinity, the man had said, but
would immediately make westward and complete the first part
of their journey the night of their escape. If the going was good
they'd reach Lough Neagh by morning, where they'd rest
up along the shore until the following nightfall. The police
wouldn't expect them to get so far and would concentrate their
searches around the coast. Besides, they'd probably also think
that if the pair were making for the border they'd take the
shortest route due south through Newry or north-west through
Derry rather than risk crossing the heartland of Ulster.

In a knotted handkerchief he had bits of gristle and meat and
crusts of bread ferreted out from the gluey mess that was the
usual meals. We want enough, the man said, to see us through
the first day. Even the second, if we can manage it. We'll keep to
the hills as much as possible. Forcing the pace, it might be the
third day before we can hunt for food.

Once on shore they would collect the guns. That would mean
a slight detour because the cache was several miles north
towards Ballygally. The man got him to explain the surrounding countryside and seemed satisfied. That was good, he'd said.

With the glens rising up almost from the sea they'd be well into them within a few hours. He wondered sometimes if the man had chosen him as a companion only because of the guns. It was a cache he hadn't told the police about when he'd been interrogated, though he'd told them about one other. That betrayal still burned inside him, and sometimes he thought of someone approaching the spot only to be arrested by the police. Or worse. Ambushed. The thought always made him break into a sweat. But as the few faces he knew to be in the same Brigade as himself never appeared on board the ship, his conscience found some respite.

Perhaps that was why he was so determined to fall in with the man's plans, to take orders from him without question. He was an old fighter, cunning and ruthless. Of that the boy was sure. You could sense it in him. The man wanted to know what make the guns were. But all he could tell him was that the cache held two rifles and a revolver. Ammunition? A hundred rounds for the rifles, fifty for the revolver. In what state of repair? Good. Lightly oiled and wrapped in sacking. He'd been taught to do that. After this piece of whispered information he thought he saw a smile on the man's face, even though the brooding hawkish countenance somehow didn't seem to alter.

And later still he thought it was stupid of him not to have mentally recorded the make of each individual gun that passed through his hands. He knew how to fire a rifle, but that was all. His job had been to collect the guns and take them to the caches. He'd been told of their exact location by a piece of paper casually slipped to him across a bar or found hidden in his bunk on board ship. Similarly whom to contact when smuggling the guns. Bringing them in, one by one, he'd sit feverishly in the room of his lodging house or in an old shed behind his home oiling and wrapping them before disguising the bundle and making towards the hiding-place. Thinking back, he recalled mostly his own loud heartbeat and the anticipated heavy knocking on the door which never came, and the hidden eyes which he was certain followed him down the street from shadowy doorways or across the fields from the hedgerows.

He'd been at sea when the civil war began, the coaster *en route* from Liverpool to Belfast. Eighteen months earlier, he had moved from deep sea ships to local ones. He was needed. And he wanted to know what was happening, and why. Though always eager to go ashore during the unloading, this time he didn't but in the evenings stood listening to the intermittent gunfire from various quarters of the city and the muffled voices that could only be riots. It was during such moments that he tried to think, standing with the cool breeze ruffling his hair as he watched the sun sink low in the sky, making the hills seem black. It was difficult to understand even part of it, never mind it all. All he knew was that this part of Ireland was still occupied by England and that now in the other part his comrades were fighting each other to see whether it should or shouldn't be. Or was that right? Was it really as easy as that? He had never had to think about his beliefs before, to turn them over in his mind to find out what he himself felt. They were simply handed on with each generation and were as unquestionable as were the words of the church. But lately a new feeling had been his. It always came when he was handling the guns, whether collecting them from his contact in England or Scotland or, very occasionally, Amsterdam, or preparing them for the cache. Sometimes he looked down the dark hole of a gun barrel and tried to think of death, of a man dying by this weapon in his hands. And sometimes he thought of the others that had passed through his hands and wondered if they had been used. It was a feeling so opposed to all other feelings and yearnings in his body, and then his beliefs didn't seem to be the comfortable protective thing they had been in the past.

He'd also thought that with each successful mission his fear and nervousness would lessen. But it wasn't like that. His awareness of his own possible arrest grew with each accomplished task, an awareness which seemed to heighten his original fear to the point where he thought he must surely give himself away by a sudden act or word. But the circumstances of his actual arrest, when it did come about, were still uncertain in his mind. Leaving a pub one night he'd been stopped by the police and taken to the barracks. There, when questioned, he'd told them that he'd stumbled across some guns hidden in the glens while doing sheep rounds between spells at sea. He hadn't told the police before because he thought they'd only believe he had something to do with them. Doggedly he stayed with the same story, though when he was interned he still wasn't sure whether they knew all about him or not. On board the prison-ship he sometimes had moments of jubilation, feeling that he had outwitted them, glad that he had played his part, however small, for the cause, glad that he'd actually done something to be interned for, knowing that many of his companions had been seized for no other reason than their name.

But such moments were rare. Boredom, frustration, fear. That was the daily reality. And when the whispered words of escape had fallen softly into his ear he'd immediately said yes, because when he tried to think of a future all he could see were bars. Huddled in the blankets at night, trying to seal every crack to keep out the chill, he carefully constructed in his mind an image of himself standing on the decks of other ships when work was done, the tang of cigarette smoke in his mouth, thinking, dreaming, watching the line of the horizon. At that time he had had a future. And no matter what he was thinking about, his thoughts always ended on the same thing. Her. His future seemed as infinite as the horizon, as did his patience. Life for him had not yet begun. Here in the cradle of the ocean his body was in suspended birth, as was his mind, his desires. There would, he knew, come a time when some revelatory moment or experience would bring him to full consciousness of self and life. It was a difficult time, standing dreaming with the sun warm on his face, lying on his bunk trying to see what darkness was and what it held, waiting to live. And in the masturbatory aftermath, which he forcibly tried to deny, though out of a strong conviction of his own being rather than some implanted code, he felt sour inside at having sullied his dream, his future, whatever its nature or shape.

'Tomorrow.'

The man strolled past him on deck, his voice urgent though soft as he uttered the single word. It was the unexpectedness of it, the now sudden imminence of the escape, which made his face and body tingle despite the mist drifting in from the sea. A quick surge of emotion, fear or relief he couldn't tell, made him feel as though he wanted to vomit and then he was calm again as he watched the man lean casually against the side to peer through the wires, his fingers seemingly manipulating something as his hands traced fleetingly along the rail. It was the inevitability which calmed him, and it was only then that he acknowledged how he had deliberately tried not to think about the escape. A wind briefly ruffled the surface of the lough, parting and rolling back the mist, and he heard the single rifle-shot from somewhere on the superstructure of the ship and watched the body roll over and lie face downwards, moving gently to and fro with the waves which buoyed it up in a watery hammock, a spectator at his own death.

He hoped that the mist would remain, and knew that the man was thinking the same thing. For him the swim across wouldn't prove difficult, though he wondered about his companion, who seemed to know so little of the sea. Once on firm ground they would stay close to the shore until the town was well behind. The lights of Larne town were now glowing through the mist, drifting with it, offering a warmth and comfort which wouldn't be theirs to take. It will be cold in the mountains, the man had said. A coldness you haven't known before.

'Tomorrow. If the dolphin comes.'

The man was past him again and going towards the ladder that led to the cages below, the voices of the guards calling and shouting across the deck. In another piece of knotted rag secreted near where he slept was grease, a mixture of what he had scraped from many plates and a quantity of engine grease the man had procured from some mysterious source. In the night he would rub it on his body, knowing that the man was doing the same. It was comforting knowing that. There in the silence and darkness his own actions would be copied exactly.

25

The grease would keep out some of the cold. All they would have when they got ashore was the clothes they wore. Perhaps even less than that, as articles of clothing would have to be abandoned if they hampered the swim. Then more would have to be found.

'Always the last to get below, eh?'

The guard's voice startled him so much that he involuntarily jerked round, gasping. The guard laughed.

'Dreaming, sonny boy? You've a long time to dream yet!'

It wasn't the guard with the kindness in his words, but another whose designs upon himself he'd instinctively read correctly when he first found the other staring at him. Ever since he'd tried to avoid him. The fist which now shoved him in the back, causing him to stumble and fall, had the brutal force of thwarted and only half-understood desire.

'Get back into your cage!'

That was the first time he dreamed of the dolphin, a dream which seemed to go on all night. It was there ahead of him, a curving sinuous sensuous shape, making for an open sea awash with splashes of bright silver. He stopped, in his dream, his nostrils filled with the fragrance of her hair, to ask her why she held the gun in her hand, because the word written on the water in seaweed spelt freedom.

In the morning the uncomfortable feeling which aroused him from slumber was the wetness smeared across his belly and thighs.

At first he hadn't thought of the boy as his companion, though he had noticed him as he'd noticed everyone. It was only when he'd eliminated most of the men that he had begun considering the boy. It wasn't a sudden decision, though when he finally did make it, after some weeks of observation, he was convinced that it was the correct one. The sturdy frame was strong, though not yet come into its full strength, the face clear and open. At times there was a kind of serenity in his eyes that contrasted with the youthful form, as though the boy's spirit was more mature than even he himself knew. But then, the sea was no weakling's life,

26

and the six years the boy had spent on the boats stood him in good stead. Yes, more than he knew. His movements too were telling, indicating reserves of power in his being as yet undisclosed. Not only would the boy not weaken, but he would willingly receive the man's imprint upon his nature. And when the boy told him about the hidden guns, that had cemented his decision. Guns they would have to have. As soon as possible. The only thing the man wondered at was the alacrity with which the boy agreed to go.

He slept lightly, undisturbed, and before rising lay for a few moments savouring the ends of sleep and conscious of his returning strength. He thought of the war. Of Collins and the ambush at Beal-na-Blath. A deep bitterness was there. That he who, above all, had outwitted the English, their intelligence forces, their army, had then to die by the hands of Republicans like himself. What had been the story filtering through the country from lips to lips? Collins in London. In signing this Treaty I'm signing my own death warrant. Had he really said that, or was it only a yarn spun after the ambush had taken place? That he had the brain to see that far ahead the man didn't doubt, his career testified to his foresight. But why then the signature? Turning, his mind drifted to an image of Childers. Childers the Englishman, holding steadfastly to the priciple of an Irish Republic, and the first to be singled out by the new Provisional Free State government to be executed. There were some things he hadn't yet absorbed.

He thought of the boy again and, uncharacteristically, leaned over to touch him reassuringly on the shoulder, smiling silently at the surprise on the other's face.

The escape went as the man had foreseen, as the boy had hoped. The dolphin appeared out of the dusky water as though summoned by a call. With the boy's quick brain, the fusing of most of the lighting system hadn't taken long, and in the semi-darkness a few minutes were sufficient to take him to the appointed spot, where the man had already withdrawn the bolts and squeezed up the wire. He slipped through and hung over the side, clinging to the rail. The man followed, pausing to pull the wire back into position, then fell after the boy with a straight drop into the water. They knew the line the dolphin invariably took and swam towards the starboard bow, the water lapping against their ears, deadening the cries and shouts of the guards above them. Now, not far over their heads, another thick wire mesh ran at an angle from the bottom of the deck rail down below the surface of the lough. The boy dived, forcing downwards while his lungs held, but the mesh was fast. Again he dived, finding no gap, an image of the dead sailor rocking to and fro on an anchor flitting through his mind and making him want to laugh. Surfacing, he saw it barely two yards ahead, a large tail, almost motionless. Silently, and, it seemed, so very slowly, it vanished, and he momentarily caught the man by the shoulder, pushing him as he himself thrust downwards once more. He swam with his eyes open, seeing nothing, feeling them sting with salt and sand, his hands as before pushing at the mesh which barred his way, and then he was swimming again, being jostled by something immense which caught him by the side and then passed him at speed and sucked him on with a fierce turbulence of water. And when next he surfaced he could tell by the distance from the ship that he was free.

Treading water, he spat, clearing mouth and lungs, seeing the man break the surface close by, spluttering and choking. Quickly he grasped his head and thrust his fingers into his throat until he vomited several times. Looking round, nothing else was to be seen except their dimly lit prison looming bulkily above them. Ducking, pulling the man, he swam just under the surface as long as his breath could last. Clearing his lungs he ducked again, after assuring himself that his companion was following just behind.

Swimming with the current they landed just beyond the mouth of the lough, closing in among the shadows of the ships and quayside as they passed through the narrow entrance, and then crawled over the pebbly shore to crouch among some rocks.

'Which way?'

The boy pointed.

'We'll give a few minutes to ease our breath.'

In the silence their harsh breathing seemed unnaturally loud before gradually quietening. The boy felt the other's hand nudge his shoulder.

'Look.'

Their late prison was fully lit again, a brilliant glare against the blackness of sky and land and water.

'D'you think they've discovered yet?'

The man shook his head. 'Not yet. It'll be an hour at least before they do. Maybe all night.' He paused, then raised himself to a half-crouch. 'We'd better start. No dallying. We want to be in the hills before they start searching.'

The boy led the way. In the water he had discarded his short jacket, though, before jumping, had tied his boots around his neck by the laces, as the man had done. They were a necessity. Now, clad only in a pullover, shirt and trousers which clung to his body, he began to shiver violently. In his intense excitement, composed of jubilation and fear, he hadn't felt cold while in the lough. With the wind now lancing against him, his body was raw and painful as he walked. Over the last few yards of inshore water he'd again had to help the man, who had been choking once more. And then he thought of that immense force he'd felt against his body and of holding the man above the surface of the lough by his hair, and was both awed and glad. Awed at the unknown, glad that the other must know that he'd been saved from drowning.

But now it was the man who ruthlessly forced him to move even quicker and soon he was sweating, his still wet clothes hardening with the layer of grease on his body and beginning to chafe his skin, adding to his discomfort. Already his limbs felt dirty and tired, and his companion's measured easy breathing mocked his own strength as he panted and gasped.

Ahead and hugging the shore lay a hamlet in an irregular line of lights. A dog barked close by, soon joined by another. Still on the shore and in the shadow of the sea-wall they didn't break their pace. Several minutes later the sombre black stone of a castle loomed out of the grey light.

The boy stopped. 'Ballygally.'

'And the guns?'

'About a mile.' The boy paused, his breathing becoming quieter. 'We'll go along the shore beyond the castle and then cut across the fields. There's no farmhouses round that part.'

The man grunted, as though satisfied. About to move off again, the boy felt the other's hand on his shoulder.

'Listen.'

At first the boy could hear nothing, then indistinctly came a whine which faded and started up again. And each time it broke out it was definitely nearer. 'What is it?'

'Wait.'

It was about ten minutes before it passed them, stopping some hundred yards behind them in the centre of the village. Silently huddling against the wall, the boy threw quick glances at his companion, recognising what the peculiar whine was as it slowly became louder and drew inexorably nearer. His companion's face was expressionless, and only once did the boy hear what he took to be a muttered curse. It was an armoured lorry used by the police, the thick grey plates on its sides giving it a squat bulk which made him think of a huge beetle, a familiar enough sight. As it passed overhead it made the wall shake, spattering grit and pebbles against his face, and he could feel a tightness in his lungs as though he was surely being crushed. It was an effort not to anticipate the commanding voice which he knew must surely come and which would make him jump out into the roadway with his hands in the air. But then he felt the man's powerful fingers grasp him by the upper arm, as if the other possessed the clairvoyance to see into his thoughts and feelings.

'A Lancia.'

The man's voice sounded like a shout before he began to understand that it was his own senses that were wrong, were distorted. Other voices broke out as the engine of the lorry fell silent, calling, laughing. He could hear them clearly. A woman's voice joined them as a door banged. Peering through a slit in the topmost stones he could see light spilling from a house and a group of uniformed figures with rifles. They were talking about Christmas, joking about it. He heard a male voice distinctly ask the woman what she wanted as a present from Santa Claus, but in such a way that her reply was drowned in uproarious laughter from the others. Sinking back on his haunches, he felt dismay seep through him. He'd forgotten it would soon be Christmas. Just as not once had he thought of these regular patrols, which he'd known were taking place, patrols that must dog their every step in the long trek ahead. He'd forgotten the most simple things, the most important things too. Across the black sea nothing greeted his eyes, no familiar comfortable object that would make his world seem real again. Not even a speck of light that would denote a ship, a warm dry bunk.

'Well?'

The man mouthed the word rather than said it, and he shook his head at the questioning gaze. Again he looked across the dark water, closing his eyes as he felt his cheeks moisten and his vision blur. On the sound of the engine his companion stood up, then motioned him to go on. They crossed the road and struck over the fields with the whine still clear in the air though the lorry was no longer visible.

'We'll rest a bit while we clean the guns.'

There was satisfaction in the man's voice. The boy had brought him unerringly to the cache. The weapons were hidden just below the ground in a cairn of stones, and as he drew them out he was a fighter again, he had once more truly become part of the war, the war that must go on whatever happened until the Republic was achieved. The rifles were a .303 and a .22, the handgun not a revolver as the boy had said but a .38 pistol of German make. He wished that the second rifle had been other than a .22, but even a .22 can kill. And the boy had said that he could use a rifle, though he hoped it wouldn't be necessary to find out how good he was this side of the border. Once over the border he wasn't sure what the boy would do. He wasn't yet moulded. There was a sense of uncertainty about him, which he disliked. For himself it was only a matter of joining up with an anti-Treaty Division.

He passed over the smaller calibre rifle and started cleaning the film of oil from the other one and working the parts, listening to the click as he tested the trigger. Finished, he pushed a loaded magazine into the socket, setting the safety-catch before turning his attention to the pistol. He stuck the handgun into the belt of his trousers and tied the ammunition pouches to his belt as well, tossing the bullets for the .22 to the boy, who hadn't yet finished cleaning it. Satisfied, he squatted back on his heels, unknotting the piece of rag which held his food, and began chewing on lumps of gristle, nodding to the other to do the same.

He had also discarded his jacket while swimming and wore only a shirt and sweater. Clothes they would need, and food. The mist, which had lifted for most of the day, began to roll back inland and he cursed it. Unfamiliar with the territory on the east coast, he'd no wish to stumble around in circles in fog-bound hills he didn't know, and hoped that the boy was certain of his bearings. The mist drifted round them, sifting the air in soft folds, and he thought of the immediate hours ahead, with the first part of their trek to Lough Neagh being the most difficult. Beyond that was his own territory which he knew intimately, as both farmer and fighter. Idly he wondered when their escape would be discovered, and where the police would concentrate their searches. He visualised them surrounding the farm and questioning his wife and children, the younger ones clinging to her, her steady voice and quiet dark eyes, patient like his own, saying she didn't even know he was free again. Her face began to form in his mind and quickly he blotted it out, not wishing his concentration to be disturbed. There was another risk in the hills, that of unexpectedly encountering a Republican patrol going to or returning from a raid. Some units must still be active despite internment. What irony to be mistakenly identified as the enemy, though, carefully considering it, he decided the chances were slim. Nevertheless, chance, the incalculable, always existed and had to be respected. Even feared, because the incalculable did not lie within his control.

He saw the boy shiver, his head down, jaws slowly chewing. He thought of the escape, when the boy had acted quickly, decisively, even to the extent of saving him. He owed the boy that, and wouldn't forget it. It was only during the incident of the patrol lorry that the man had sensed his state of near panic. But that hadn't surprised him, coming as it did in a prolonged moment of inactivity with his body still charged with a surfeit of energy. That was one thing he'd have to teach him. How to react properly to events. How to be able to summon all his energy in a second, how to keep it lying just below the surface of his being and at the same time feel relaxed, how to use it economically. How to avoid the wastefulness of tension, of fear. There was no place for them. They were like hate, he'd learned a long time ago. The energy expended in hate was energy totally wasted.

As he stood up he transferred the pistol to the left hand side of his belt and grasped the .303 in his left hand, feeling the length of wire wrapped round his wrist chafing his skin as he did so. It was the wire he'd used on the bolts. After freeing the bolts he had unthreaded the wire and tied the ends together to make it one long piece. They'd need it for rabbit snares in places where a gunshot was too much of a risk. The .22 could be used for hunting, and then he thought it was a good thing they had it with them after all.

'Which way now?'

The boy carefully looked around, but the mist had closed in further and he couldn't even get a glimpse of the sea through the thick shifting folds. He pointed to his right. 'We came from that direction. From the sea. So up there must take us into the hills.'

'What time do you think it might be?'

'It was about four when we jumped ship.' He paused. 'About nine, maybe.'

'Yes. About that. Remember. In this first stretch we want to be at Lough Neagh by daylight. You lead.'

He watched the boy walk up the gentle slope, keeping close to the low stone wall, the rifle dangling from his right hand, ammunition pouches attached to his belt as the man had shown him. He followed him, keeping about a dozen paces behind, a feeling of well-being and joy seeping through him at this present mission, which could have been any other of an infinite number of missions. Truly he had joined the war again. He looked round for landmarks, but saw nothing but clumps of shrubs and the gnarled form of a tree leaning through the mist some way above them. The baaing of sheep occasionally eddied through the darkness.

After about an hour he stopped the boy, who pointed vaguely in front of him. He knew that the boy was uncertain of their position, but pushed him on nevertheless. To stop would unnerve him further. A compass was what they needed, even a watch so that they could at least judge their pace and how close was daylight. But that was asking for a miracle.

The two men who suddenly loomed between them were talking so loudly that for a moment he thought they'd been challenged. He raised the barrel of the rifle as one of them moved his hand to his gunbelt. 'Don't. Or I'll kill you.'

The four figures stood, silent now, the mist threading between their bodies.

It was the older man who spoke. 'Who are you?'

The man took in their every detail, forcing his thoughts. 'Slip off your coats and kick the gunbelt over here.' Then, as the coats fell to the ground, he asked, 'Where's the other gun?'

Again it was the voice of the older man. 'He isn't carrying one.'

'Where are you going?'

'For a drink. The pub.' The older man's voice was steady, testing him. 'Don't you know where that is?'

For a moment the man was silent, looking from one to the other. If the village was still just at their back then they'd been stumbling blindly round and round it.

'You won't get far.'

He stared into the eyes of the older man, his voice non-chalant. 'Maybe. Maybe not. On you go.'

'Where?'

'Where do you think?' Tying the gunbelt round his waist and

34

transferring the rifle to his right hand, he said, 'We've good contacts in these hills and well you know it. By the time you get back down the glens in your bare feet we'll be in another county. If any of you try anything we'll shoot without hesitation. And we'll take our risks of still not being caught. Go on.'

Still they paused, as he threw one of the greatcoats to the boy. He motioned with the barrel of the rifle and they turned, the younger of the two men taking the lead. It was a bluff he was counting on, a bluff that they thought he and the boy knew exactly where they were. And it was working, he thought, feeling the ascent becoming steeper and the breathing of his companions more laboured. Then they were suddenly out of the mist into a landscape of dark rolling hills under a sky heavy with stars. Away behind him he saw a pale thick band which he took to be the sea.

The older man paused. 'Here?'

'Another few miles to the west. And then you can give us your boots and start hobbling.' He tried to smile. 'When you get to the pub you can ask for a footbath as well as a pint.'

But there was no smile on the faces of the two men as they turned and started walking again. He studied them as they moved ahead of him, at the same time motioning to the boy to keep well away to their left with his rifle pointing in their direction. The older man was in the uniform of a police sergeant. Obviously a regular. His companion was wearing a police jacket and cap, and civilian trousers, no doubt one of the Special reserves, those voluntary groups who assisted the main force. And who were out more for vengeance than for keeping the law, according to the tales he had heard. But to all tales he gave a wary ear. He listened as they talked softly between themselves, and suddenly made his decision. Now it was only a matter of deciding upon the place to carry it out.

They crossed a few smaller hills and then climbed a steeper one. Standing on a ridge he knew that this was the place. He called to them and they stopped, and all four stood looking across the bleak lifeless land.

'Slemish,' the boy said quietly.

35

'Good.' He turned to the policemen. 'Take your boots off.'

As both men bent down he cracked the older man across the back of the head with the butt of the .303 and, before the other could untangle himself from untying his laces, had the wire pulled from the gunbelt at his waist and wound round the other's throat and was knotting it, feeling him clawing at it and hearing his choking gurgles of terror. In a few moments he let the lifeless body slither to the ground.

The boy's voice was tremulous. 'You said—'

'Shut up!'

But now the boy was lunging at him, his voice sharper. 'But you said—'

He waited till the boy was nearly on him, then hit him sharply across the face and, when he tried to speak again, hit him a second time. Then he pulled him towards the corpse. 'Strip him. Of everything.'

From the sergeant's pockets the man took wallet, pencils, report book, pipe, tobacco and a police whistle. There was also a pocket-knife with a curved blade, razor sharp. The wallet contained personal items, photographs and ticket stubs, and a police identity book showing the owner to be Sergeant Duncan McKinzie. It also held four one pound notes, and in an inside pocket of his waistcoat he found a heavy silver watch. Peering into his face the man judged him to be well over fifty.

By the time he'd satisfied himself with the sergeant, the boy had stripped the corpse. Boots, socks, underwear, trousers, shirt, pullover, jacket and cap lay in a heap. He instructed the boy to get into the clothes, even though they were much too big for him, then stripped himself naked, tying his own still wet clothes in a bundle before buttoning the sergeant's greatcoat tightly round his naked body and strapping on the gunbelt with the .45 slipped into the holster. The boy was now walking up and down, ungainly and comical, trying to become adjusted to his new garments. Quickly he rolled the corpse into a sheugh, pulling stones and bracken and grass over it.

As he squatted back on his haunches he noticed the sergeant watching him.

'Why did you kill him?'

'We needed his clothes.' The man paused, his voice softer. 'We could only take one. Two of you would've been too much to watch. And we couldn't let either of you go back down those hills.'

'Take to where?'

'Donegal.'

'And you've dumped him over there?'

'Yes. Over there.'

The sergeant crossed to where the corpse lay and brushed the flimsy covering aside. Tenderly he stroked the young man's dead face, shutting tight one eyelid that was barely closed, his fingers tracing the red weal at his throat. Watching, the man thought he heard a choking sound, but when the sergeant spoke again his voice was clear and steady.

'You'd leave him here for the crows to pluck at? It could be months before he's found. If ever.'

'What do you want? A minister?'

The sergeant's voice was barely audible. 'No. Breath for him.'

'He's past that now.'

The sergeant didn't reply. He knelt, almost cradling the corpse in his arms.

The man stood up, pointing the barrel of the rifle at him. 'You're our prisoner. Our hostage. It's time to go.'

Slowly the sergeant stood up, and to the boy's eyes his frame seemed to blot out the sky as he stood tall and bulky and massive, his unshaven chin flecked black and white.

'Hostage I might be. But I'm not going anywhere till he gets a half-decent burial. And you'll have to use that rifle. Because I'm damned if you'll be able to truss me like some chicken.'

They stared at one another, the man's eyes momentarily squinting and disturbing his otherwise impassive features, as though there was something he suddenly knew, understood. He abruptly turned away, coming back a few minutes later with several pieces of slated rock, which he tossed to the sergeant and the boy.

'Start digging.'

Working fast in the soft earth they managed to make the grave nearly three feet deep. The sergeant took the boy's wet shirt and wrapped it around the head and shoulders, then placed the body in the ground and covered it up, using two small twigs as a cross. Before leaving the man closed over the black gash in the earth with boulders and stones and bracken so that it looked like any other natural formation to the passing eye.

As they stepped over the ridge to the other side the boy took a last swift glance, his guts still in a sickening swirl, knowing that his face was tense and white, seeing the pale naked form of the young man rising up from the stones, the terror stricken lines cutting deep into his face and eyes and his fingers clawing at the scarlet band gouged into his neck.

Art

We go down the slopes of Slemish almost running, the sergeant
between us and in front. I am on his right, the man on his other
side and slightly behind both of us. He wants me in his sight too.
He doesn't trust me, I know, even though without me he
would've got stuck in the mesh under the ship and wouldn't
have known about the guns. He holds the rifle in his right hand
and out from his body and has it pointing towards us.

Many times I turn to look back up the hill where the constable is buried just under the ridge. I don't mean to. If he
hadn't bumped into us just like that he'd be in the pub now with
his mates. I can't stop thinking about that. I can still see him.
His face. Dark hair he had, with blue eyes and a round smiling
face. A glensman too. Like me. Easy to tell that. Doing the
sheep rounds mostly and working the land. The ground is
harder as you dig down and the slate keeps breaking. And the
man saying—That'll do, that'll do, the crows haven't got
shovels in their claws. But the sergeant doesn't answer him and
just keeps on digging. And after a few minutes the man says—I
could put a bullet into you here and now an' it'd be your own
grave you're digging and I wouldn't even have to push you into
it. But the sergeant doesn't say anything to that either, and goes
on scooping the earth with the broken slate and his hands
bleeding and his face black like the soil.

The body lying beside the hole looks so soft and weak. Like a
bit of putty. It doesn't look like a man somehow. Even a fish

39

when you haul it into the boat splatters about to tell you it's living and has been living. But not the body. It might never have known anything. The thick red ring round his neck is the only mark. And his tongue was hanging out a bit. His cock was shrivelled up so's you could hardly see it and I wonder if he's married. Or if he's known what it's like with a woman. You shouldn't have to die without knowing that. I watch as the sergeant puts his tongue back in and closes his jaws, then pulls the eyelids down. I give him the shirt to wrap the body in and then he takes the policeman's badge from his cap and puts it on the white chest. It lies, harp and crown and the red hand of Ulster. As I help him lower it into the grave he purses his lips and prays and then looks at me and gives me a quick smile and I find I've been crying. I can feel his hand touching my face as he says—Good there's someone to cry over his grave. Ashes to ashes, he says, turning away again. Then I watch him walk over and look into the man's face and say—We are all ashes. But the man avoids his eyes and goes and stands on the ridge as the sergeant makes a tiny cross. Then he comes back to pile some boulders on the place to cover the signs of digging.

We stop on the next ridge, panting and dragging our breath, with the man looking round the hills and then at the sky. The sergeant sits down, his fingers kneading his calves.

'Is it a race you're running, mister?'

'We've got to get as far as we can before they start searching,' the man says.

'As far as you can from where?'

'The *Argenta*.'

The sergeant nods. 'They'll be missing the other one by morning. And me.'

'And they'll find us easier than they find him.' The man pauses, again looking round the hills. 'Do you know this country?'

'Well enough.'

'We want to make the top of Lough Neagh before daylight.'

'And what happens if I lead you straight into a police barracks?' the sergeant says.

'You'll die and we'll take our chances at staying alive.'

He stares at the man. 'It won't be the fear of my own dying that'll stop me. You can be sure of that.'

The man's voice is harsh. 'Well? Where from here?'

I watch the sergeant strolling round for a few minutes and then he stops. 'We're a bit further north than Lough Neagh.' He stops and again studies the land and then I know why the man's been closing me out. I told him I knew the land but I don't know it like the sergeant does. I got us lost in the mist. And then I think if I hadn't got us lost maybe the constable would've still been alive. If we'd been well away from the village as we should've been then they wouldn't have bumped into us like that. I look at the sergeant wanting to say—It's my fault that he's dead, it was really me that killed him. But my tongue won't speak.

'I take it you want to keep to the hills?' the sergeant says.

'Yes.'

'Keeping roughly straight you'll come to Lough Beg.'

'And you too.'

The sergeant only nods.

The man motions with the rifle for us to move on. 'That's even better,' he says. 'And don't lessen the pace. We've time to catch up on.'

We start running again but the going's too rough for that and we slow to a fast walk. The ground's slippery and our boots sink into it. It's then I think of the dolphin for the first time since clawing at the mesh underwater when I was stuck again. That crash on my side. It was the dolphin that hit me through the gap. It must have been going out through the hole too. Out to freedom.

'They'll shoot you if they catch you,' the sergeant says close to my ear. 'Or maybe you'll be lucky to get away with being locked up again.'

For a minute I think he's talking about the police, and then he says, 'It's the Free State that'll win. They'll control the country. The Republic's nowhere in it.'

I wonder how the sergeant has guessed right and move away

from him and turning a bit I look back at the man to see if he's heard anything, but his face is set and he says nothing. I meant to ask him that when we were on the ship, about what we'd do when we got to Donegal. Finding the right army can't be easy. But his face mostly stops you from asking anything. It makes you feel afraid just to speak. Now I know why I felt glad when he was floundering about in the water. I'm afraid of him. Just the way he killed the constable. So silent. Quick. And you think of death being long and slow. Just putting the wire round his neck without anyone seeing what was happening. Or knowing even. No fuss. Like the sergeant said. A chicken. Just like wringing a chicken's neck. I killed him too.

The sergeant slows so that we come up on him and I see the man poking him in the back with the rifle barrel.

'What's wrong?'

'The pace's too fast for me. You forget you can give me about twenty years.'

'You'll go as fast as I tell you to,' the man says.

The sergeant laughs. But it's a strange kind of laugh. Like there's tears in it. 'Then you'll have to leave me behind,' he says. 'And you forget too. I'm not used to taking orders from below my rank.'

It's funny the way he says it and I laugh too, but stop again as the man stares at me.

'What rank are you?' the sergeant asks.

'It's nothing to you.'

The sergeant laughs again, but softer. 'I still can't go any faster. Not even if you're Michael Collins himself. Were Michael Collins.' He stops for a minute. 'Before your kind shot him.'

I see a twitch on the man's face but he doesn't answer and stands looking across the dark hills. It's then I'm aware of the sergeant like the way I was back at the grave. His height and big shoulders stand over me and I look at his thick hair, black and grey, sticking from under his cap and the grey showing in his beard. His face is broad and friendly and there's a scar on his right cheek and I wonder what fight he got it in and if he has killed anyone. Then I notice he's watching me too and turn my head away.

'Know this, mister. Don't forget what I said. If you're thinking of killing me too you'll have to use that rifle. You'll not jump me like young Ned. There'll be no wringing my neck like some squawking turkey.'

His voice booms out, making me jump a bit. Then I smile. The way we think of the constable's death as the same thing makes me feel close to him. When I look at him again he smiles too and winks, but I turn away. The man is still staring into the darkness, silent and like a statue so that you have the feeling he isn't with you and I wonder why the sergeant with his bulk doesn't try to jump him. I lift the barrel of the rifle up and think of the dolphin.

The sergeant laughs again. 'What rank's the boy?'

'Shut up.'

From his pocket the man takes the watch he lifted from the sergeant early on.

'Don't lose it,' the sergeant says. 'It's my only heirloom.'

I know his voice is directed at me but this time I keep turned away from him.

The man puts the watch back. 'It's near four. Daylight's about eight.'

'We'll make it,' the sergeant says and starts walking without the man telling him to. I follow him, taking up the same position behind him and to his right, knowing that the man is following in his old position though I can't see him.

As we move inland the mist clears and now the sky's bright and starry with a moon. After a while I hear the man call and find I've somehow drifted close to the sergeant without knowing it. I move away, smarting at the man's voice. But it doesn't seem real now. All that of jumping from the ship, hiding behind the sea-wall, has gone. The excitement. The gun in my hand doesn't seem to belong to me.

I can feel myself tiring fast. The soft ground sucks the boots in and holds them. And the constable's clothes are too big. They fold into creases and cut into my side. When I get my own dried

I'll throw his away and only keep the jacket against the wind. The greatcoat too. When I think of his clothes like that it's as though he's still alive, even though I can see his white body lying beside the hole on the ridge. It didn't have to be done. Then I wonder what he'd say if he knew I was wearing his clothes and look back a couple of times with a feeling that he's following us. And then I laugh because that's stupid. I think maybe it's the tiredness that's making me nervous and I begin to whistle softly and see the man walking towards me.

'Sounds carry a long way,' he says.

I don't answer.

'What're you thinking about?'

I shrug my shoulders, not knowing what to say.

'The policeman back there, isn't it?'

'Yes,' I say, not meaning to say anything.

'If we'd taken two we couldn't have completed the trip. Two and only two of us is open to danger. And if we'd let him go then in a few hours there'd be a thousand on our heels hunting us.' He walks beside me not speaking for a while. 'Maybe you'll know what killing's like yourself soon. And maybe with the sergeant. He's a hostage. But some bunch we happen to run into might have little notice for a hostage.' He stops again. 'In fact, we might have to do that anyway if he keeps slowing us up the way he's doing.'

The man moves away from me as the sergeant turns and beckons, and I follow. Day is breaking behind us and there in front is a long pale stretch like a ribbon. Water.

'How far?' the man asks.

'Four or five miles maybe.'

The man agrees. 'Seems about that.' He turns and looks round the hill and then points to a cluster of stunted trees near the top, and says, 'Up there. We'll wait till night again. They'll soon be up and about down there and there's no point in risking being seen.'

He's right. A few minutes later a light shines from a huddle of cottages. We stand watching it before the man walks away across the hill, motioning us to go to the clump of trees. He

44

returns in a little while to tell us there's a stream at the other side. He takes my rifle and stands over us as we wash and drink. In the centre of the clump of trees there's room enough for two bodies.

'You two sleep,' the man says. 'I'll take first watch.'

He shakes out his bundle of clothes and lays them on the grass to dry, as I've done. Then he takes off the sergeant's greatcoat. Though I know he's naked underneath it still surprises me and I watch as he kneads and cleans himself all over with fistfuls of dewy spiky grass, a picture forming in my mind of a chalky body with a red ring round the throat.

I wake up with the same picture in my mind and the man's foot kicking me in the legs. I stand up and stretch. The short day has already passed and it's dusk again. I put on my own clothes though they're still damp, and start digging a hole.

He watches me. 'What are you doing?'

'Burying the constable's clothes. They're more of a hindrance now.'

'Tie them into a bundle. We might need them yet. Besides, we don't want to leave anything behind so soon.'

The hunger in my belly is savage now that I've moved about and I untie the knotted handkerchief and start eating the bits, giving some to the sergeant, who's awake and beside me. But he spits them out almost at once.

The man looks at him. 'That's the muck we have to eat on board that ship.'

The sergeant says nothing, but I hear him spitting again as I go to the stream and drink and wash the sleep out of my eyes. When I get back the man is lying in a small hollow with the greatcoat wrapped round him, several yards from the trees. The sergeant's revolver and the rifle are close to his hands and in clear view. 'Waken me at eight. That'll give us another twelve hours' going. And stay away from him,' he says, nodding towards the sergeant. 'If he moves towards either of us, shoot.'

The silence is long and loud. I get cramped and begin to

45

move about, sometimes walking round and round before sitting
again with the rifle across my knees. The man doesn't move.
Only his hair and part of his face show from under the coat.
Neither does the sergeant, who sits with his back against a tree,
his head sunk into his chest. My mind keeps drifting to times
other than sitting on this freezing cold hillside and I keep
jerking back to the present moment in case the sergeant jumps
me and gets the rifle. I put my finger on the trigger, thinking I'll
just shoot blindly if he does because that will waken the other
one.

'Are you a Republican?'

The sergeant's voice is a whisper. I think for a minute.

'Yes.'

'What kind?'

I don't know how to answer that, and shake my head.

'This one here. He's a fanatic. You can see that. Are you
going to die with him?'

I shake my head again and get up and walk around, but the
sergeant's voice follows me.

'Well, lad?'

Again I just shake my head.

'I saw many of you die. I was in the south and only came back
up here when the civil war started.' He stops again. 'And no
war's worse than civil war. Family against family. Brother
against brother. Fact.'

'Shut up,' I say. But my voice has no force in it.

'To die not knowing the good things in life.'

A long silence follows. But his words keep whispering in my
ears, maybe because they're my own thoughts too and I'm
trying to hide them from myself. It's then I remember I dreamt
about the dolphin again, when I was curled up in the constable's greatcoat. And a girl. But I can't remember anything
about them now. About what they were doing. What I was
doing. They were just there. Side by side.

His voice whispers another time. 'Well? What kind of
Republican are you?'

'I don't know,' I say truthfully.

46

'Then you'd have been better staying on the ship. At least you wouldn't have been shot there.'

His words are true, I think. Because now the bars of the prison-ship are like the rifles I can't see coming behind us, coming all round us and making the dark rolling hills seem like an even bigger prison. And the gaoler makes me afraid every time I look at him. In his sleep he hardly moves and I can hear his deep breathing. I wonder about him, about what he thinks, and once more tell myself I should have got to know him before we escaped. But again I know I couldn't have done that. When I asked anything his eyes just seemed to shut himself farther away from me. I jump at a noise and quickly jerk the rifle up.

'Steady, lad,' the sergeant says. 'I'm only easing these old limbs.'

I watch him get up and stride up and down, and then he opens his trousers and there's a splashing sound on the grass. He sits down again, his legs straight out in front of him.

'How old are you?'

'Nineteen,' I say.

'That was Ned's age.'

Even though I know who he means, I still ask him. 'Ned?'

'The one you and me buried up on the ridge on Slemish.' He goes quiet again, then says, 'A great one for the lassies up the glens. And for the fishing. They say here in the north we've got the best salmon rivers of any place.'

The surface of the water splinters like thin glass as their broad backs push and jostle against each other going upstream, arcing over the leap, tails flashing, making for the sheltered pools to spawn. I used to watch them for hours, not knowing why. Dreamy, it was. Like you were floating in the stream with them. It was like that with the sheep in winter. I round them up with the dog, get them huddled tight to warm each other and then sit in an old hut with blankets round my shoulders and a small fire, watching them press together and climb over each other. Alone in the hills wasn't lonely. There's all the world to think in. To dream in. Dreaming of a girl naked and soft like the snow. And the yearning in you that is everything and ends in a wet muzzle nudging you and the sheep bleating they want to move. I suppose Ned knew all that too. Him lying up on the ridge. Knew more. In the snow in the glen a girl naked and soft. Funny. Now he's dead I almost know him. I who killed him too.

A shriek sounds. It rises suddenly and stops, startling me, and I stand up. Though short it had terror in it, agony. Ned died almost silently, I find myself thinking, and look towards the man where he turns slightly under the greatcoat and is still again. Again I think of us on board the ship. In the cages we hardly glanced at each other. There was only the whispering between us when we were exercising on deck. I don't know him at all. Maybe that's why I feel afraid of him.

'A rat.'

'What?'

'That sound,' the sergeant says. 'Or could be a rabbit.'

'Yes,' I say.

'It was a death-sound. You can tell.'

The silence is long after that and I keep shuffling the rifle in my hands, putting it down and picking it up again. The sergeant sits with his head sunk back into his chest and I think he's asleep. But I'm wrong.

'You're a seaman?'

'Mostly,' I say.

'Good life for a boy.'

I chafe at his words and speak without meaning to. 'Man.'

He chuckles a bit. 'All right, lad. Man. Ned was like that too.'

Ned again, I think. It's strange. As though he's with us on this trek too. And then I wonder why I think like that.

'Been far?'

'Mostly just round the coasts, this past year or so,' I say, thinking of some of the ships I've been on. 'Scotland. England. But I've been deep sea too. Africa. The East. Spain.'

'Spain, eh? The dark-eyed beauties with the sun in their blood.'

I look at him. 'You've been there too?'

'Italy. The women there are the same. During the war, it was.

48

The world war.' He's quiet for a while and then turns towards me. 'I've seen too many wars, son.'

'Have you ever seen a dolphin?'

He shakes his head. 'Why?'

'It's just . . .' I break off and we are silent.

'I know,' he says. 'Sometimes things are hard to put words to. Some things can only be described in silence.'

'In the sea they're beautiful. The other week I saw another one over by the lighthouse at Port Patrick. You can feel they're with you. Are for you. It's like seeing a beautiful spirit.'

The words just come out but then they seem silly and I turn away so that he can't see my face.

'A beautiful thing, son. To have eyes to see like that.'

I'm not quite sure what he means and feel awkward, so I quickly laugh. 'A seaman's yarn has it that they're the souls of dead sailors.' I'm about to tell him of the dolphin and the prison-ship, and stop. It would be like betraying something. Something sacred.

'And how did you join up with this one?' the sergeant asks, pointing to the prone figure.

'He just asked me if I wanted to escape with him and I said yes.'

'And no regrets so far?'

I don't answer. 'When were you in the south?'

'In Belfast for a short while. Before that in Cork and Dublin. When the old Irish Constabulary was disbanded I came back to join the RUC. Back home.'

I try to joke. 'So you're hardly a Republican.'

He turns towards me, thinking as he speaks, his voice low. 'What's in a word, son? If I knew what kind of a Republic it's supposed to be then I'd know whether I was one or not. And God only knows what kind of government's going to come from this bloody mess now going on. But that doesn't mean to say I like England any better than a lot of others. Not some of the things she's done and doing still. The Great War taught me a lot of things and this war's teaching me them again. Like the churches. One sure way to lose respect for the church is to see the clergy on either side shouting us on to have our guts spilled out. It was like that in the trenches too. But at least here in the north if we disagree with the church we can tell it to go to hell without being damned for it. So what am I? An Irishman. But a northerner.' He stops for a while. 'We're just a small country far too close to others more powerful than we are. That's been our trouble. Too many meddlers.'

He stops again and stares at me and I feel uncomfortable. It annoys me too the way he keeps calling me son, though I know he probably doesn't mean to. He probably doesn't even know he's doing it.

'That's the only good thing about war,' he says. 'It makes you ask questions. Why you're fighting. Killing. And you, son? What makes you so convinced a Republican?'

I shrug my shoulders, still not knowing how to answer him, and he's silent again. I look at the sky and wish I knew the names of all the stars and think maybe that's one of the things I'll do when I go home again. Get a book of the stars and learn them. Then on deck I can pick each one out and call it by its name. Doing that brings things closer. Like the dolphin that time with the herring. As if it was swimming in the stars. The ones I do know, I draw lines joining them together. The north star. The Great Bear. Venus. The evening star. Venus. Venus.

'What would it be like to die?'

It's my own voice, though it doesn't sound like me. That's what I used to do when I was alone with the sheep in the hills. Talk out loud. Talk to them. Your own voice sounds funny in the hills. Speaking out loud with no one to hear. Not that the hills are silent. They talk all the time. But theirs is a different kind of voice. Like the sound of rain soft on the grass, falling softly.

'Now how would I know that?' he says.

'Know what?'

'What it's like to die.'

I'd forgotten I even asked it. In a group of stars I trace the outline of a dolphin. It's swimming fast, leaping, leaping from a silvery wake. Venus.

'Or maybe I do,' he says. 'Are you afraid?'

I turn and look at the man again as he moves under the greatcoat. His left hand grips the revolver, then eases. Then I remember he gave me the watch before lying down. I slip it from my pocket. It's after seven o'clock. In an hour we'll be moving again. I go down the hill a bit, crouching, and look towards the cottages where there's a few scattered lights and beyond them the gleaming flat stretch of water of the lough. In the towns they'd have the evening papers by now with news of the escape in it. And pictures too, maybe. Arthur McLaverty. Tidg O'Donnell. I can see my mother close to the fire, sitting wondering, the excited faces talking in the pub, telling stories of how the escape was done. But none of them know.

I stroll back again, and sit a few yards away from the sergeant with the rifle across my knees. If we have another good night's going we'll be in the Sperrins by daylight, I remember the man saying. The way he speaks of the Sperrins makes me think that it's like a place where he feels no one can find him.

'Look.'

I follow the sergeant's pointing finger to where a large hare is sitting on a tuft of grass just the other side of the trees.

'He'll make a good dinner.'

'I might miss,' I say.

'Here, like this.'

The sergeant crawls over beside me and takes the rifle from my hands as I keep my eyes on the hare. Then I lie alongside him as he takes slow aim as it moves slightly and squats again, nibbling. The sound of the rifle is sharp but not loud and the hare half-leaps and falls on the grass.

'Put the gun down.'

The man's voice is steady, but I feel a kind of violence in it. He's crouched naked, the greatcoat thrown aside, the bigger rifle pointing directly at us.

'We've got a good bit of game for eating,' the sergeant says, dropping the gun and walking towards the hare.

'And we're game if anybody heard that shot.'

The sergeant comes back, dangling the hare by its hindlegs. 'What? A .22? In these hills you'd have to have pretty good ears

51

to hear the sound of that rifle at all. You know that as well as I do.'

As I pick up the rifle the man comes towards me. The first blow hits me on the right side of the jaw and I fall, tears spurting from my eyes at the suddenness of it. As I get up his fist hits me on the other side and I fall again.

It's the sergeant shouting, though I can't see him. 'That's enough!'

The third blow hits me on the chest and I kneel on the grass, sucking in my breath, my hands gripping my thighs. His voice is as savage as his fists when he speaks again.

'Never let your gun out of your hands at any time. Understand? Never.'

As my eyes clear I see him move away, still naked, carrying the rifle. He lifts the greatcoat and drops the revolver into the pocket and goes up the hill towards the stream. The immediate pain eases from my body and I can hear splashes as he washes himself down. The sergeant begins to come towards me, but I wave him away. The man is returning as I too go to the stream, but he passes without even looking at me. A wind has sprung up and is moaning through the trees here and there. Shivering, I slip off the pullover and shirt and bury my aching face in the stream till it's almost numb, feeling weak and dizzy even though I know my face is flaming like a fire.

When I come back the sergeant has skinned and gutted the hare. He looks up at me.

'All right?'

I nod, but say nothing.

The man appears, slipping two rabbits from wire snares which he must have set that morning while we were asleep, and as he pulls them from the loops I think of Ned.

'We'll keep the hare for tomorrow night,' he says. 'By that time we should be well into the Sperrins and might risk lighting a fire.'

I watch as he cleans the rabbits and cuts the flesh from the bones in long strips. Then he divides out three parts and nods for us to eat, but I shake my head.

The sergeant holds a piece in front of me. 'Eat it, son. You'll be in need of it.'

I think I'm going to vomit but all I can taste is a thick cloyingness. We chew silently, the man tying up the remains for later in the night. He digs a small hole and buries the bones and skin and puts a stone on top. Only then does he dress, in his own clothes again, and I wonder how he can stave off the cold. He tosses the greatcoat to the sergeant, who puts it on without speaking. When he sits down again he has a packet of cigarettes in his hand and he gives me one.

'These were in the other one's pocket. Which you didn't go through.'

I didn't, I recall. And then feel glad I didn't.

He hands the pipe and tobacco to the sergeant. 'We could do with a luxury. But keep the flame hidden.'

'We could do with more than that,' the sergeant says, filling the pipe.

As I light my cigarette from the match in the man's cupped palms I feel his fingers lightly brush the swellings on my face, but he says nothing.

We wait till the last light in the village has gone out, and then another half-hour, before going down the hill with the sergeant in front.

Three

With the night the wind rose higher and brought the rain horizontally across their path to cut into exposed faces and hands. They passed to the north of the village with only the barking of a dog to tell of their presence. The surface of the lough was dark like the land, sometimes glinting near the shore as the wind serried it. Soon even the greatcoats were sodden and from the soft ground large lumps of earth clung to their boots, making the two figures in front stumble. The sergeant fell, and the boy stooped to help him up again, their hands holding on to each other for balance.

The man joined them, his voice loud so that they could hear above the wind. 'Slow the pace. We don't want either of you to risk a broken leg.'

The sergeant wiped the mud from his hands with grass. 'We won't get far tonight.'

'We'll get far enough. We have to. Go on.'

As the others moved forward the man took up his position at the rear. He could hear the sergeant wheezing even though the pace was half of what it had been. The boy walked, head down, barely two yards behind him. It was really too close if in an unexpected moment the sergeant decided to jump the boy. And for all his protestations of being an old man, there was power in that huge frame yet, a strength that would make the boy's undeveloped body seem puny.

But the man knew that an incident like that wouldn't take

place. Nor was it just a guess. He'd sensed it first when, from beneath the greatcoat, he'd watched the two lie side by side as the sergeant took aim on the hare. His own rifle had been in his hands, the safety-catch off, with only the eye of the barrel protruding from under the coat. There'd been a gentleness in the sergeant's voice as he spoke, showing the boy how to hunt.

And he'd sensed it again when he hit the boy, hit him not out of anger but just as a lesson in what not to do. Never let your rifle out of your hands. There was anger in the sergeant's voice when he'd shouted, anger at some code of his own being broken. They were very different men.

No. The sergeant wouldn't jump the boy. More. He wouldn't try to escape. For some reason of his own he had decided to undertake the trek with them. That was good. It made things easier as he could be trusted to some degree. But what worried the man was not knowing the other's reason.

As they passed Lough Beg he mentally recorded the fact that they'd crossed the boundary into County Derry. With luck the police and army would still be searching Antrim and south to Belfast, thinking that they might try to lose themselves in the city. But the sergeant had been right. They wouldn't make much ground on this part of the journey. The land in front of them was low and saturated with autumn and early winter rains. He cursed as one leg sank to the knee in the spongy earth and he found himself having to use the butt of the rifle as a crutch to haul himself out, knowing that the others were watching. Calculating, he thought that at best they'd make some seventeen or eighteen miles. But that was enough to bring them to the high ground at Slieve Gallion and the beginning of the Sperrins. They'd spend the next day there. And the next night would see them into Tyrone and well into the mountains, where the going would be faster. The important thing was that they'd made good ground on the first night. More than twenty-five miles, he reckoned. Time stood to their stead.

'A break?'

The sergeant was squatting, the rain shining on his red, heavy seamed face.

His eyes slitted, the man stared around the black fields, but could find no cover. 'All right. But let's find some kind of shelter. There's no good sitting here, totally open.'

In about an hour they found it, a cottage, like many others, long since abandoned, with only two walls intact. Part of the thatched roof was still in place, showing patches of grass. One gable wall had fallen inwards, littering the interior with boulders. Scrambling over them, they found the south-west corner to be dry. Their eyes becoming accustomed to the heavy light, they worked to clear a corner. Taking off his greatcoat, the sergeant hung it from a rafter, then removed his boots and started picking clay and earth from them with a stone. The boy did the same. The man watched them for a moment, then sat with his back against a wall, his rifle standing beside him.

The sergeant fumbled in his pocket. 'All right for another pipe?'

Preoccupied with his own thoughts, the man barely nodded. Then, tossing matches to the sergeant, he passed a cigarette to the boy. In the dank air the acrid smoke gave the feeling of warmth.

'And where do you think we are?'

The man was silent for a while. 'Ten miles from the Tyrone border. Maybe twelve.'

'And where do we go from here?'

'Into the mountains. The Sperrins. It'll make better going.'

'North?'

'West.'

The sergeant sucked on his pipe. 'You're right. There'll be too much activity round Derry.' He paused, squinting into the man's face. 'That was a smart move, bringing Derry city into the northern boundary.' He paused again, longer this time, waiting for the other's reaction, but none came. 'Why don't we stay here till the weather breaks? It's only dragging the guts out of us.'

The man sat drawing on the cigarette, saying nothing. Abruptly he stood up, beckoning to the boy. Outside he turned his face to the wind and rain, listening, but no other sound came. Already the landscape was growing visibly clearer, and he checked the watch. Progress had been even slower than he'd thought. He cursed, returning the watch to his pocket and making up the steep slope behind the cottage, the boy following.

From the top of the slope they watched daylight slowly bring the land to life. The cottage lay at one end of a long valley. Half-way down the valley was another, but even from this distance he could see that it was abandoned also. In his mind he peopled it with figures, half-consciously stroking the rifle. This was partly what the war was about. Centuries of abandoned cottages, hovels, because they afforded no living and never would afford a living when not under the people's own control. Centuries of exiles, making north and west for ships to America, to anywhere. From the cottage he watched them walk away, a bundle on their shoulders, a pig under their arm. Their wealth and warmth. How many deaths had been averted on the coffin ships in the freezing ocean gales, when man or woman had huddled close to a pig and lived by its protective warmth? A good beast. A wisdom of the soil to be made brutal mockery of by the ignorant. The thought buoyed up his feeling of tiredness. At the other end of the valley he could make out cattle, and beyond that again, the mountains. The land on the other side of the slope was the same, giving the feeling of being uninhabited.

'You're getting too fond of that old man.'

The boy looked quickly up at him, but didn't reply, though a flush appeared on his face.

'He's our enemy and would kill us if he had the chance. When you've a gun in your hand it's not a person you're shooting at. Just someone who'd kill you. Like the ones he's killed. Like the policeman I killed.'

The boy's voice was unsteady. 'We killed. I did too.'

The man stared into the boy's face, but it showed nothing as he kept his eyes fixed to the ground.

Back in the cottage the sergeant asked, 'Well?'

'We'll stay the day here. But you'd better get good rest because we'll have to make it up in the night.'

They ate the remains of the rabbits, chewing hard on the

tough raw flesh, before the boy and the sergeant rolled up in a corner. He hung the hare on a rafter and, taking the boy's rifle along with his own, went outside. Soon he'd found a few rabbit runs and, with the wire, set four snares. Surveying the land yet again for any other sign of human life and finding none, he brought down two wood-pigeons with the .22. Satisfied, he cleaned them and hung them beside the hare, and went outside again.

The weather broke. About noon the rays of a weak sun were splashing across his face as he sat outside the cottage, thinking. Once into the mountains, should he go north for a spell? That would bring him near the farm. He could make a brief visit. The police would hardly be watching it constantly. There he would find news of how the war was going. That's what bothered him most. Knowing absolutely nothing about what was happening. He knew that on board the prison-ship he'd heard nothing but rumours and deliberate lies. And if the sergeant's words were to be trusted then the Republic was rapidly being defeated. Another defeat. Yet never defeated.

And what was the sergeant's reason for being with them? Because it was now obvious to him that the other had decided to be one of them, decided to see the thing out, even though he knew the chances were it would be his own death too, should they run across an army or police patrol who'd decide to fight it out, hostage or not.

And the boy. When he'd said that this morning—We killed. I killed too. What did he mean? What was he including himself in? The war?

And then he remembered when he'd been trudging through the rain he'd been thinking about Childers again. The Englishman who'd died for an Irish Republic.

The sergeant was the first to waken and he rolled over, wincing at the pains in the joints of his legs and arms. It was dusk again and he wondered momentarily whose the voice was that was talking to him. It was the boy, babbling softly about a dolphin and the sea. He smiled, reaching out to touch the boy's face, which was hot. Stroking the forehead a few times, he pushed himself into a sitting position and then stood up, hitting his head against the dangling hare.

The man was sitting just inside the cottage, hidden from the slope, a rifle on each side of him and the sergeant's revolver in his lap.

'The boy's beginning a fever.'

The man didn't move. 'So?'

'We should do something.'

'What?'

The sergeant paused, suddenly aware of the stupidity of his statement.

'This little army doesn't afford a field-hospital.'

Looking down, the sergeant scrutinised the other's face. It was the first time the man had displayed any wit or sarcasm, shown any hint of humanity behind those deep eyes almost hidden by the brows. 'There's that hare. We could boil it. Make a broth of some kind. Make something hot. At least it will help.'

'All right.'

Again the sergeant paused, taken aback by the unexpectedness of the agreement.

The man stood up. 'Some of those rafters'll be dry enough to burn. And as this was once a small-holding there must have been plots among the grass. There just might be something worth digging up. The only thing is something to boil the stuff in. But we'd better do it quickly.'

Among some junk in what had once been a shed the sergeant found an iron pot and with small pebbles and grit scoured the inside clean. There was a stream to the east of the cottage, the man told him. By the time he'd washed and filled the pot and returned to the cottage a fire had been lit in a circle of stones. Balancing the pot across the flames, he watched as the man cut up the hare and pigeons and tossed them into the water. Outside again, he slowly traced round the dilapidated buildings, eyes keen to any sign of what once might have been cultivation. Sifting through the rank grass and turning over the soft ground with his hands he eventually found potatoes and carrots and turnips, and cut away the pieces still fit enough to eat.

The man had returned to his usual position, sitting on the ground with his back against the wall, guns close at hand.

'You were right about the vegetables.'

'There's always something to eat if you know where and how to look. Even in barren land.' He paused. 'But then, it isn't barren, is it? Only to some.'

The boy was still sleeping, still occasionally babbling.

The sergeant looked at him, then stood over the prostrate form to feel his forehead. 'Why so much about a dolphin?'

'Maybe it's a beautiful dream,' the man said.

By the fire again the sergeant slipped the pieces of the vegetables into the now boiling water. 'How long do you think it's been abandoned?'

'This place? About twenty years. Thirty, maybe. Probably in one of the great drifts to America. Though it seems it's been used since. Tinkers.' He paused. 'Gunmen. As they're called.'

The sergeant stirred the broth. 'Salt's what we need.'

'Well, if we were nearer the sea we could get some of that too.'

Poking the fire, the sergeant glanced sideways at his companion. The man hadn't moved. There was only the voice, speaking slowly, deliberately. But he wondered about this sudden communicativeness.

'Why do you stay with us?' the man asked.

'Stay?'

'With me and the boy?'

'Amn't I your hostage?'

In the lengthy silence the sergeant waited, evenly stirring the broth, occasionally glancing at the figure motionless by the wall.

'I mean your reason.'

'None other than you've got a gun.' He paused. 'Four guns.'

'I don't believe you.'

The sergeant said nothing.

'You an Antrim man?'

'Yes. Above Larne. You?'

'Tyrone.'

The sergeant nodded. 'That makes us both Ulsterman anyway.'

'Whatever that means.'

'Like the Republic? Whatever that means?'

Now the man was silent, offering nothing.

'Perhaps you're right,' the sergeant said. 'Maybe death is the only meaning. Your own. Someone close.'

The man moved, as though to stare at him over the glowing ashes of the fire, the sergeant thought. But his face remained expressionless.

'Why don't you accept the Treaty?'

'Because it'll leave us just where we were before. Especially here in the north.'

The sergeant nodded. 'I wasn't always stationed in the north. Saw some bad times. And I was still in Dublin when the civil war began.' The sergeant paused, waiting to see if the other would answer. 'The Free State government's been ratified. Just before you escaped. And they've got the money and the guns. More than your side has.' He stopped again, but as the man didn't answer, asked, 'What happens if there's no war to join by the time you get to Donegal?'

Suddenly the man stood up, lifting a rifle in each hand. 'Fill the boy's belly with as much of that as you can. We'd better move.'

'And what if he can't go?'

'He'll go.'

Taking the pot from the fire, the sergeant tried to waken the boy. Breathing heavily and talking incoherently, he was slow in becoming conscious. He wiped the boy's face and hands with the sleeve of his pullover and raised him into a sitting position. Using a slim flat stone, scoured clean, he ladled the broth into the boy's mouth, tenderly holding him round the shoulders, until the pot was half-empty and the boy's splutterings told that he could take no more. The dying glow of the fire showed up the flush on his face and the unnaturally bright eyes.

Turning, the sergeant saw the man standing silently behind

him, in his hands two empty snares and another two with a rabbit in each. 'How is he?'

'Not good.'

The man motioned to the pot. 'You'd better have your helping.'

The sergeant drank slowly, sucking at the pieces of meat and vegetable. Judging that he had taken about half of the remainder he passed the pot across and watched as the man simply opened his mouth and poured the contents down.

'All right. Put the fire out and scatter anything we've used. But bring the pot. We've lost enough time.'

The sergeant's voice was insistent. 'I tell you I don't think the boy's in any shape to go.'

But the boy was fully conscious now, though unsteady. 'I'm ready to go. Who says I can't?'

The man held him by the shoulder as he staggered. 'How do you feel?'

'All right. It's only a cold that's made me dizzy.'

'You needn't take a rifle. I'll take both.'

As the man turned he paused and looked deliberately into the sergeant's eyes for several seconds, then left the cottage.

They went up the slope, now with the boy and the sergeant side by side, the man following. The break in the weather of the afternoon had remained. And the wind had changed quarter. The sergeant felt it fan his cheek, drier, crisper. That meant that in the mountains there'd be frost.

He stayed as close to the boy as he could, his hands instinctively reaching out when the boy stumbled, his eyes frequently searching the boy's face to see if there was any change. Twice he turned round, silently indicating that his companion now needed a rest. But all the man did was to point the rifle to say go on.

He hadn't got the man's measure yet, the measure of his being, the measure of his being a man. There in the cottage he'd tried unsuccessfully to get him to betray some of his feelings but was only made more aware of a sense of inviolability in the man's every movement. That he was an old hand as a fighter, had often seen action since the guerrilla campaign had gained momentum after the World War, was certain. That's why he had talked of being in the south, of being in Dublin when the civil war began, to get him to open up, so that even as enemies they had something to share, even if that something shared was talk of battle.

Yes, he had been in the south, and in some of the places where the fighting had been most vicious. And with a British withdrawal and an Irish Provisional government imminent, it seemed natural to return north and join the RUC. But in a sense it was a step backward, back to a war which he'd left.

The boy stumbled and fell and as he helped him to his feet he again turned to the man, but the latter still shook his head and pointed the rifle on. And it was then that the sergeant felt a deep and bitter anger overwhelm him, a feeling he'd been aware of but was careful to hide. It was perhaps even hatred, he thought. He turned quickly, holding the boy, hoping that the darkness had concealed the expression he knew to be on his face.

But when the boy fell again several hundred yards further on some of the emotion broke through his guard. He pulled the boy up and held him against his side, feeling the dead weight of weakness, waiting until the man approached.

'Are you going to kill this one too?'

His voice should have been cold and deliberate. That was the way he wanted it. But it wasn't, and the betrayed intensity only angered him further still, making him shout.

'Are you?'

'Carry him.'

'He'll die.'

'He'll take his chances like you and me. Carry him.'

The sergeant watched the barrel of the .303 curve up to prod him in the chest.

'Carry him as far as you can. Then I'll take him.' The man pointed to where a mountain was outlined against the clear night sky. 'Slieve Gallion.'

'Up there?'

'Yes. We'll soon be in Tyrone. And we'll keep to the mountains.'

The going was difficult with the boy clasped across his chest and half-hanging over one shoulder. Several times he paused to rest, but the man didn't now urge him on. They were climbing steadily, the land falling away on all sides. Sometimes he tried to think, to concentrate, but the body bobbing against him continually broke his concentration and all he was aware of was his own plodding feet and the thought that he would soon collapse himself.

'All right. I'll take him now.'

The sergeant laid the body on the ground and stretched his aching shoulders and arms, watching as the man rolled the boy up in the greatcoat he'd been wearing and effortlessly draped him across one shoulder. Still with a rifle dangling in each hand, he nodded to go on.

Relieved of his human burden, the sergeant suddenly felt the going remarkably easy. The softness was being taken out of his muscles, they were beginning to take the strain again. He smiled at the irony of it. That it was a trek like this which was bringing his body into the condition it should be.

Three times he tried to engage his companion in talk, but without avail. The other strode swiftly and silently on, never breaking his pace, as though contemptuous of his load, causing the sergeant to wonder at the strength packed into the long stooping frame. Having spent a lifetime among men in similar circumstances, he judged this to be an uncommon power and in his anger and hatred there was admiration, even a feeling of kinship.

Daylight seemed to come more swiftly in the mountains than it had done in the land below. The dun-coloured landscape suddenly opened in front of them was vast in its emptiness, for the sergeant the criss-cross pattern of dark stone walls heightening the sense of loneliness, isolation. The work of hands long gone. It was easy to imagine a people vanished, leaving only this to tell of their passing, the brooding stone weathering wind and rain. From a ridge he gazed into the dusky length of a valley, seeing nothing, the shadows and darkness not yet totally dispelled. Further on he paused, his eyes beginning to pick out details, the browns and greens of different soils, a purple clump of late heather, white streaks of frost. Here and there sheep strayed. The steamy vapour of his own breath bathed his nostrils as he continued to survey the land, gradually becoming aware of a mood of gloomy melancholy now settling on him. During the trek so far he had simply been intent on the moment at hand, carefully guarding himself from other thoughts and feelings which threatened to upset his fragile equilibrium, and had nearly done so once or twice. An intense desire for some sign of habitation swept through him, and involuntarily he held out his numb fingers as he saw himself standing in front of the big range of the farmhouse which was his home. Abruptly he turned. 'How's the boy?'

The man was also looking across the land with the boy, still wrapped in the greatcoat, on the ground beside him. He didn't turn as he spoke. 'Still alive.'

Quickly the sergeant crossed and looked into the other's face, trying to keep in check the anguish and bitterness building up inside him. The chalkiness of the young features was streaked with colour round the eyes and temples. First blowing on his hands and feeling the sensation of returning circulation he checked the boy's pulse, noting the heat rising from the sweaty dampness of his body.

He stood up. 'What now?'

But the man ignored him, standing silently as though at one with the dark stone.

They were on the ground then, the heel of the man's left hand forcing back the sergeant's neck. Behind the blindness of savage rage which blurred his sight he could feel the muscles round his throat straining, twisting. He blinked and saw the dark snout of his own revolver a few inches from his face. They lay like that for a few moments, and then the weight from his body was removed as the man swiftly rolled away and stood up again. Rising also and retrieving his cap, the sergeant noticed the line of blood down the other's jaw. The skin round the knuckles of his own right hand was torn too and as he licked the salty sweetness he wondered at his only being able to half-remember his driving the blow home, so all-consuming had been his anger.

'The worst of the fever's on him now,' the man said. 'If he lives the night he'll do.' He paused. 'But we'll not keep him alive this way.'

With the throbbing in his knuckles and the steady ache creeping into the muscles of his neck came a sense of shame. The other was right. He'd allowed his control to go. To go stupidly. Without purpose or plan. And in the confused welter of thought and sentiment and anger loomed another face, another pain, and a vague numbing hatred of this land he loved to call his own. Yet his voice was steady when he spoke. 'Well?'

The man nodded upwards. 'A few miles to the west there's a dugout. We'll hole up there. That'll be shelter for him.'

The man's eyes were steadily holding his, probing, and the feeling of shame grew more acute. There was something else in those eyes too. Some new feeling lay between them. But of what the sergeant wasn't sure.

'Normally you would've been shot.'

The sergeant laughed. 'Normally?'

'You know what I mean.'

The nervous ripple of laughter had gone almost as quickly as it had come, leaving the same feeling of gloomy despondency which had been with him before the incident had happened. 'I know what you mean,' he said, and turned towards the boy.

'No. I'll take him.'

The man wrapped the greatcoat more tightly round the recumbent figure, using the belt to tie the bundle across his right shoulder. When the man moved the boy's feet bumped against his thighs but the sergeant called, 'Wait!' With the belt of his own coat he strapped the boy firmly to the other's body. 'That'll make it easier for him. And you.'

The man's voice was gentle. 'We'll soon be there.'

He moved off again, walking quickly, both rifles now carried in the crook of his left arm, leaving the sergeant to catch him up, as though in a silent acknowledgement of trust that now the latter would make no attempt to attack. The sergeant accepted the gesture and came abreast of his companion a few yards to his right, so that the other would have him in view. They kept a steady pace, gradually gaining height, not once even seeing a farmhouse, something which he interpreted as being that the man was now in his own territory and knew it intimately. It was close to noon before they stopped and the boy was unstrapped and laid on the ground. Some fifty yards away lay a knoll, thrusting precipitously up from the long gradual slope they had been climbing.

'Wait here,' the man said.

Rolling a boulder to where the boy lay, the sergeant sat down, wiping the sweat from his brow with the cuff of his sleeve. The figure in front disappeared over the knoll, and he was alone, listening to the incoherent babbling of the boy in his delirium. The name of the prison-ship was repeated several times, mixed up with the talk of a silver dolphin. Idly he wondered why the two things had been joined together. It was like dreaming, he thought, when physical boundaries were shattered and there was only the intensity of sensation. The prison-ship he'd seen many times, yet hadn't really seen it. It was there, floating boxlike on the water, a functional object of war. But here was the reality, a spirit driven to escape whose end was possibly nothing more than raving on a mountainside. In his mind drifted the small cross he had placed on another mountain, and he was again aware of a hatred of his own origins. And now it was as though he sat watching different figures capering in this wilderness in mad ephemerality like some composite lunatic John the Baptist, laughter bursting loudly from him as he saw himself part of this macabre comedy, the face of a circus clown pasted over his own as he stood in this desert beating his breast, guardian of a mad boy, while another sought a hole in the ground for them to hide in, to hide from the savage avenging angel whose face was their own suffering no longer mute. Looking up, he saw the man watching him silently, the .303 slung across his naked torso, the whiteness of his body framed against the sombre earth, and he laughed loudly as before.

The man looked at the boy, then him. 'Well?'

'I suddenly saw him as being very funny.'

'The boy?'

'God.'

The pictures ceased to be, those murky shadows flitting in and out of his mind. Suddenly the sergeant felt very tired. 'The dugout?'

'Just over the rise.'

He struggled up as the man slung the boy over his shoulder and began climbing. A path zig-zagged across the face of the knoll and he slipped and scrambled up, crawling over the top on his hands and knees as an attack of dizziness made the mountains and sky swirl in front of him, holding tightly to the clumps of tough springy grass for fear of sliding back again. Behind a straggly wind-beaten copse lay the dugout, a broad trench still partly covered by branches. The man had already lowered the boy into it, and was kneeling beside him unfastening the greatcoat. He followed, half-smiling, fatigue crushing him to the earth like a stone.

The man turned, then rummaged among the clothes he had discarded the first time he'd climbed the knoll. Producing a bottle, he tossed it to the sergeant. 'Here.'

The liquid was cloudy, and foul, yet he was glad of the burning sensation in his throat and belly. Though he didn't want to, he laughed again. 'Miracles?'

'Foresight.'

He took another gulp of the poteen and handed the bottle back. 'Not the best I've tasted.'

'The best prison can afford. But we might have better before long.'

The boy was naked, the man rubbing and chafing his skin with a piece of rough cloth until it began to glow. The fever was still the same, as the high colour on his face showed. A long heavy shirt was pulled over him and then he was wrapped in blankets, the man pouring some of the poteen into the partly open mouth, holding his head as he coughed and spluttered.

'You sleep,' the man said.

'And the boy?'

'I'll see to him.'

Scooped out of the side of the trench were large cavities, the floors composed of sacking and straw, remarkably dry. The sergeant crawled into one, relieving himself only of his great-coat, which he then pulled over him, aware of his conscious mind beginning to drift almost at once. He lay on the edge of sleep, hearing the man's movements and the moanings and babblings of the boy, his mind, in odd moments, weaving patterns round the sounds, though patterns of familiarity, barrack-room and home. He was a long time in struggling out of sleep and equally long in remembering where he was, as though some deeper urge had obliterated the past three days from memory. Pain came with a vision of the grave on Slemish, and with the rest the same overwhelming weight of fatigue. Crawling out of the trench he saw that it was still daylight. In these short days of winter, dusk would come in mid-afternoon, which meant that he had hardly slept at all. The floor of the trench had been brushed clean. In an adjoining sleeping-place lay the boy, now quiet. As he crept back into his own he noticed the smaller rifle standing upright in a corner. But there was no sign of the man.

He awakened again with an acrid smell in his nostrils that was vaguely familiar. The fatigue had gone, and he lay stretching and feeling the energy flow into his body. It had been a long time since rest had been so luxurious. His mind was sharp too, awareness of present circumstances coming immediately. He first went to the boy, who was still asleep, though otherwise he showed no change. In the sheltered half of the trench an oil stove flickered, set between two stones. A grill was placed across the stones and on this a pot bubbled. He bent closer and sniffed deeply. Herbs. Though quite what he wasn't sure. A remedy as old as the land itself.

The night was quite dark, only a few stars showing briefly between breaks in the cloud. He noticed the two rabbits lying limply over the lip of the trench as he climbed out, and the .22 standing in the corner as before. Accustoming his eyes to the darkness, he followed the sound of water to where a spring broke over some stones several yards away. Further down he relieved himself first, then returned to wash slowly, feeling the last vestiges of sleep vanish.

At the trench again he paused, listening intently, but no sound came telling of the man's presence. Lowering himself in, he went to the stove and stirred the contents of the pot, then tasted it. It was bitter and thick, reminding him of sour broth. The .22 was in his hand before he consciously thought of lifting it. He cradled it in both hands for a moment, then deliberately returned it to its former position before taking the knife which lay beside the stove. Leaning over the trench he began to skin and gut the rabbits, thinking that the only real discomfort at the moment was in his mud-caked and sweat-stained clothes, waiting and listening for the man to come back.

The man didn't return during the night. The sergeant waited a long time before cutting the rabbits into strips and putting them over the grill, every now and then forcing some of the herbal stew down the boy's throat. He cut the meat into smaller pieces and fed that to the boy also, wondering if the man would be proved right about the latter's survival. Then he slept again, waking only to satisfy himself about the other's condition. Sometime after dawn he inspected the dugout, finding more blankets, oil for the stove, tinned beef, a variety of ammunition. He bathed at the spring again, stripping himself naked, his skin tingling in the cold morning air, noticing the several irregular lines running down the knoll from the trench. French drains, which accounted for the dryness. It was a good site. Several men could hole up here for a long time. Patiently he waited, his thoughts taken up with the trenches in France of a few years before and the long lines of attacking German infantry.

It was mid-morning before the man returned, appearing suddenly over the knoll, rifle and large bundle over one shoulder. He was wearing different clothes, heavy cord trousers and a thick sweater, the sergeant noticed. There would be plenty of places in these hills in sympathy with his cause.

'How's the boy?'

'Still alive. And his colour's down.'

'He'll do.'

'But hardly able to travel yet.'

'We'll see.'

The man knelt and untied the bundle, tossing across underwear, shirt and sweater. 'These might feel a bit more comfortable.'

The sergeant nodded. 'If I'd known you were going to be away all night I might have taken the chance to scarper.'

The man stared at him with the same probing look as before, then asked, 'Would you?'

'I didn't fancy a bullet in the back and nobody up here to bury me.'

'You had the opportunity.'

True. And in a mildly surprised way the sergeant recalled that not once did he think of escaping. It seemed natural to stay, natural to look after the boy. And again the man was hinting that he had known he wouldn't try. 'What's the news?'

'It's Christmas Eve.'

He felt uncomfortable under the man's stare, and tried to adopt a jocular tone. 'That's the reason, then. I declared a truce. Don't all good wars have a truce at Christmas?'

'Not this one, it seems.'

The man's voice was intense. What news he had gleaned obviously boded no good for the Republic. Fleetingly the sergeant felt the strangeness of his position, fighting in a three-sided war yet not belonging to either of the main parties.

'Did you miss this time?'

'Miss?'

The man nodded towards the .22. 'I thought you might have done some hunting.'

'With an empty gun?'

'It's loaded.'

Dropping into the trench he lifted the rifle. The other was still watching him intently, his own rifle held across his knees. Climbing out he stood looking over the land. 'I'll do it now.'

'Here.'

He caught the small pouch of extra ammunition in mid-air.

'Use as little as you can. We don't want to tell the world we're here. Just in case a patrol of the wrong sort is about.'

The sergeant abruptly turned and walked away, almost feeling the other's gaze at his back. Some fifty yards away he stopped with a sudden desire to turn and look, but didn't. It was some kind of test, he knew. His eyes traversed the barren expanse. Was he free to go? Or was it a ruse so that the man could bring him down with a single shot just like the game he himself was hunting? As a hostage, was he really necessary any longer? With the boy recovering, they could be over the border in a few days. And, with the man's knowledge of the terrain, only a stroke of ill-luck could make them run foul of a patrol. Escape now meant that he could have police and army patrols all over these hills by the following day. But in the ensuing gun-battle there was every chance the boy would die, and that he didn't want to happen. Besides, if he didn't go back there was no knowing what the man would do. Perhaps hole up in another dugout or similar place which no amount of searching would uncover, or strike out in an entirely new direction. In him the sergeant had sensed the cunning and ruthlessness of generations who had fought both for the land and the land itself for survival. But there were yet other reasons and desires for staying. His own. Not even half-understood, they clogged his being. So far he had guarded himself from thinking about them, afraid of what he might say, or do. And now, his strength having returned after the long night's rest, he felt the bitterness and hatred well up again.

It was after dusk when he regained the trench to toss a solitary hare on the ground beside the man. 'That's all I could get.'

The man picked it up and examined it. 'Good enough.'

'Decided when we're leaving?'

'In a few hours.'

'With the boy in that state?'

'We won't be going far.'

'Where?'

The man was silent for a while. 'My home.'

'That's where you were last night?'

'That's right.'

'With us left out on the mountain? The boy?' Caustically, the sergeant added, 'Some war. When you can go home in the middle of it and leave a prisoner to nurse a sick youth.'

The blank mask habitual to the man's face momentarily broke, the sergeant noticed with satisfaction. For the first time he had managed to penetrate his guard.

'It's that kind of war.'

'True. Hardly the Western Front.'

'More vicious. But without the big guns.'

'But with its home comforts. I might as well keep these fresh clothes till I've had a warm bath.' The sergeant paused, changing his line of attack, trying to force his initial advantage. 'And how's the Republic doing? Well but not alive?'

The man didn't answer, but began gutting the hare. Then he asked, 'Are you a hostage?'

The sergeant ignored him and jumped into the trench. The boy was still sleeping, the high colour almost totally gone from his face. He crept out of the sleeping-place, his voice softer. 'You were right about the boy.' As the other again didn't reply, he said, 'And if the police make a raid?'

'They've already been. And maybe won't return for a while. I doubt if they'd think I'd run for home so soon. Anyway, we'd have plenty of warning.'

'Still, it's a risk.'

The man shrugged. 'We'd be away. And they'd hardly do anything to any of mine.'

'You mean not as you did to the one on Slemish?'

The man wiped the blood-stained knife on the grass. 'Let's clean up. Home comforts, as you say. At least you can have your hare at a warm fireside.'

But the sergeant was insistent. 'Well? Slemish?'

The man turned as if about to speak, then suddenly climbed out of the trench and made for the spring.

In about an hour the dugout was back to its former condition. The sergeant, with the boy strapped to his back, watched as the man adjusted the tarpaulin and the last of the branches and grass. They walked silently, each sunk in his own thoughts, until the man made a gesture to wait. Some minutes later a light shone through the gloom, which the man answered with a soft barking sound. It signalled again, twice. Following quickly on the heels of the other, the sergeant saw a long, low cottage loom out of the gathering darkness and the bright glinting eyes of a dog, black like the earth, and the tall form of a woman standing in the soft glow of the doorway.

Tidg

They were waiting. All of them. Her. The young ones. The dog Shane. Instinct, it was. Approaching down the sloping fields to the back of the cottage and seeing the two glints and then the shadow move black against the black of night. It fair shook me inside and why? My own dog, isn't he? Come to greet me out of the darkness silently as I taught him to. The barking and leaping are for the fields and the sheep and daytime. I kneel and feel the cold nose against my hand, the warm tongue on my face. The sound of a door opening and I hear her calling him. His head turns and he pauses, unsure. I push him gently and nod for him to go on and watch him go towards the house, with the backs of my hands wiping the wetness from my face. Her bulk moves into the yard as the dog reaches her and still kneeling on this patch of stubborn earth I feel the pulse of my life and hers. Crying. Crying alone.

A barn door is hanging on a single hinge, the door I meant to fix before they took me. I notice other things, grass underfoot through the flags where it shouldn't be, the ridge of thatch at the chimney at the wrong angle, meaning it's thinning and falling away. It always goes there first. Even at night there's things to be seen, noticed. I am glad. Glad to feel the workaday rhythm of these hills tingle my skin as though I'd never gone.

I try not to startle her but fail. I speak softly yet distinctly; she turns at the sound of my voice with an exclamation and a soft oath and I feel her body falling against me. Not in an embrace but in shock. Her arms hang limply for a moment and then she steps back. Now I see the wetness of her own face and hear her faltering voice, and I become aware of the guns, the rifle in my hand which a moment before I didn't feel, the pistol in my pocket and the revolver in its holster, and it's as if I am violating her and this place that is her home.

Inside I lean the rifle in a shadowy corner and go to her again as she stands before the range, poking the smouldering turf into a glow. We lean against each other. Not in passion, desire, nor even affection. But like two beasts of the field that huddle together for warmth, protection, or for some more obscure need.

'There's two policemen missing.'

'Not now,' I say. 'Don't ask.'

She pulls away from me, repeating what she has said. Her voice is angry, harsh. I stand silently as she pulls a pot across the range. She's ready to lash out, to hurt, to demand. I can sense it. Such acts as this are a kind of violation. I understand that where years ago I didn't. I was ignorant then. Perhaps am still.

'You'll be hungry.'

Just as if I'd only come in from the fields and not trekked across half the country, ears intent for the sound of my pursuers. She moves away with a deliberate step and I stand a stranger in her home. Familiarity comes slowly. It comes first with the heat seeping into my body and bringing to my senses the comfortable smell of a cottage in winter after heavy rain. A smell of damp earth and mortar. I sit in the armchair to the right of the fire, the dog resting his head on my thigh. Above me are three shelves lined with books and I reach for one just as I've always done on those nights when there's an hour to spare. It's Davitt's *Leaves from a Prison Diary*. In Derry I bought it for a few pence. But now I can write my own, I think, and smile at the idea.

As I sit, I'm aware of something out of place, something new, and only then see the small tree in the corner draped with coloured paper and tinsel. Sprigs of holly hang from the low-beamed ceiling. Tomorrow will be Christmas Eve. I had forgotten that. A sound makes me turn and I see the young ones at the foot of the stairs with the wee girl Maeve already running into my arms, her laughing scolding childish voice just as I'd heard it inside my head during the days of captivity. She's warm in my arms, her hair and sleepy body musky like a young pup. Her mother comes in from the kitchen, rebuking her for being out of bed. My own voice is stern as I ask the two boys why the barn door is hanging off, why the yard is unkempt. As they stand shuffling their bare feet I think that they're big for their age, thirteen and eleven. Soon the older one will go. A farm like this can't feed too many mouths when there's little work on it for more than one. Where will he go, I wonder. And then briefly such thoughts are pushed aside by a picture of the other boy lying in the dugout. It unsettles me, and I force myself not to think of him. I must savour these moments. When I leave again these will be my food.

With the children back in bed I strip and wash and put on the clean clothes laid out. Sitting by the fire supping stew I wait for her to speak, still sensing the strangeness between us. It was like this other times I was away, but not so deep. It's an agony like my own, an agony which I can share with no one. There was no time of innocence. My inheritance.

'You'll stay?'

I know she knows that the question is foolish. 'No.'

'Where will you go?'

'Donegal.'

'The Republic will be defeated.'

'I must go.'

Her voice is flat, passionless, but that is not her will, I think.

'Who's with you?'

'A boy.'

'Only a boy?'

'And a policeman.'

'Two went missing after the escape.'

I don't answer, and she doesn't ask again.

'You'll stay the night.'

About to say no, I stop. It's not a request. 'The boy has a fever.'

77

'And you left him out on the mountain? Would you do that to one of your own?'

'If need be.'

She rises heavily, putting her hand on my shoulder. The clasp is firm, but tender. 'You can't be broken, Tidg. You can only die. And what am I to do when they bring you home to me dead?'

From a chest she takes a bundle of newspapers and drops it into my lap. Newspapers carefully solicited, I know. I reach out to her, but she brushes past me.

'The Republic's already defeated,' she says.

'It can't be. It's our beginning.'

She stops on the stairs. 'And bring the others in for a day. There'll hardly be police come on Christmas. The boy. The boy's to be brought in.'

'Have the police already been?'

'Once. But they said they didn't expect to find you here.'

Sitting alone, I bend to her will. I think of the sergeant and the boy on the mountain, and go to the window. The night sky is overcast, though a few rifts in the cloud appear as I watch. It will remain dry, I think. The sergeant will be waiting for me to return. By now he has seen the .22 I left. Deliberately. A momentary fear passes through me as I think he has all night to travel in. It was a test, leaving the rifle. To see if he truly stays of his own will, as I believed he would. But that's when I thought of being away only an hour or two. A night is a long time and a man can waver, revoke a decision. Still, I think, it will test him all the more. Yet it makes me uneasy, the unexpected coming into it. Her demand. I am half-way to the door, rifle in hand, when her restless feet overhead make me pause and then return to the newspapers and range.

I leaf slowly through the pages, weighing item against item. On the day of our escape British troops begin to leave Dublin. Power is being handed over. But not to the Republic. It is the Free State which is fact, which is law. And the execution of Republican prisoners continues. Just as in the war against the British we are being forced back into the hills and mountains.

My mind strays from the printed page as I visualise small bands of fighters going to ground throughout the length of the country. Waiting. Creeping out to attack. Just as before yet not as before. There's one item that I don't wish to see and I leave the newspapers aside and sit staring into the fire, the warmth making me aware of a feeling of weariness that is not physical.

In bed she lies away from me. Sleep comes quickly, but a troubled sleep. I carry the boy and the sergeant down a hillside. Both are dead. The creasing pain in my side is from a bullet, and I waken with an echoing sound in my ears.

Her hand is on my forehead, soothing me. 'You were talking. Crying out.'

'Saying what?'

'Nothing. Just . . .'

Just a cry. Nothing else. I sleep again and am floundering in the water. Drowning. Crying out for the boy and the big fish. I break the murky surface of the lough and am awake again. Yes. I was saved by the boy. She moves closer, her warmth spreading through me. I turn into her, afraid.

Up before dawn I sit by the window as light spreads across the hillside. I notice a few moving specks and carried on the wind is the sound of a church bell. Sunday. The figures are those trekking to Mass in the next valley. In the kitchen the boys are getting ready to go and I warn them to say nothing. Not that I believe they would, but it seems a necessary reminder none the less. She bustles around us, preparing breakfast. 'What about the wee girl?' I ask.

'I'll keep her here. She can go with me tomorrow. Christmas Day.'

Today is Christmas Eve. Again I'd forgotten. 'I'll need some clothes,' I say.

'For the boy?'

'The man.'

'You'll come back?'

I say nothing, and watch my sons making ready.

'God keep us from shooting on Christmas Day. You'll be safe.'

I leave the cottage quickly, taking the guns and the clothes she has given me. Her hand is on my arm, and I nod. I don't go far. Only far enough to be out of sight in hiding. I want this, simply to observe my own home. I watch my sons trudging up the far hillside to vanish over the lip. They'll come back by a different route having covered miles in the hills to see that the sheep haven't strayed too much. The wee girl comes round the back of the house with the dog Shane. He stops once or twice, looking up towards me. But there's no betrayal. She comes to the door to look up also for a long moment, then crosses the yard to unbolt the henhouse. The first two are seized in a wild fluffing of feathers and she disappears round the side of the cottage. In my mind I see her, the large firm hands cleanly snapping the necks. She appears again with the limp carcases ready for plucking. What am I to do when they bring you home to me dead? This. So it will be when I am not here. If I'm not here.

The sergeant watches me coming. The .22 is undisturbed. I toss him the clothes and then see to the boy. He'll live. I know the sergeant is watching my every movement, and in our quick exchange of talk we warily circle round each other. His face betrays nothing as he lifts the loaded .22. Did he really not check it? I toss him more ammunition and he goes off to hunt, disappearing quickly over the ridge. Finding a different position I wait, my own rifle in my hands. Some time later I hear a faint rifle-shot carried on the breeze, which means he has made no attempt to circle and ambush. Uneasiness comes then, fear. His presence is now like a threat, as if it is I who am the hostage, the prisoner.

He returns through the fading light with a hare and at once asks about leaving, his words challenging me, because of the boy. I say we're going to the farm, my home, so that the boy can rest. So that the boy can rest. That's where I was last night. To see if it was safe. We can rest up in comfort for a day and night before making the second part of the journey. It being Christmas too. But the sarcasm in his voice is deliberately probing my resolution, and again the idea of who the hostage really is crosses my mind and I challenge him on that, but he turns away without answering, going to the boy. I hear him behind me, talking softly, indistinctly, and I half turn, blood dripping from the knife where I'd been skinning the hare, aware of the rising violence inside me like a trap ready to spring. But he's beside me again, talking about the boy, about the police, his own kind. And of our safety, as though he were one of my own. I say that even if they did come we'd be well out of the way, so it doesn't matter. I can feel the threat again as he speaks of the other policeman on Slemish and for an instant it's in front of me, the naked body with the bruise on its throat and the cairn of stones fashioned into a grave. An image of war that gives me back my balance, my authority. An image of what might be me. I wipe the knife on the grass and tell him to clean up the dugout.

We don't speak after that until we reach the farm. At the door of the cottage I unstrap the boy and lay him in front of the range, then beckon to the sergeant. He comes in, his bulk filling the doorway, and stands uncertainly watching my wife. It's she who breaks the lengthy silence, telling him to make himself easy. But he just stands watching her as she fills a basin with hot water and begins to strip and bathe the boy, talking softly to him all the while. He's half-conscious now, his eyes roving round the room as he tries to grasp his whereabouts, and again I think of the lough and of floundering, lung-filled with dark water. I owe him a life.

'Give me a hand.'

The sergeant bends at her voice, helping to wrap the boy up in blankets. I watch this ritual that I so often performed, but now as a stranger, and the morning comes to me of sitting on the hillside watching my own home as though I no longer belonged to it. I search the sergeant's face for signs of hostility, but he's completely engrossed in his task. He takes the boy from her and nods for her to show the way. As they climb the stairs I unload the rifles and slip them behind a large dresser that practically covers one wall. I slip the ammunition into a pouch and hide that also. The pistol and revolver will stay with me.

She is behind the sergeant as they descend the stairs. 'You'll both want hot water too.'

'The children?' I ask.

'I've told them not to come down.'

'The boy?'

'In our room.'

'The sergeant and I will be sleeping down here.'

The sergeant spreads his hands out in front of the range. 'No need to stay out of your bed. I'll do nothing.'

She quickly glances at me, her expression questioning, and I become even more aware of the strangeness of the scene. 'Just the same. I'll sleep down here.'

'Your choice. But for no good reason.'

She stares into his face. 'Why are you like this?'

'I've no choice. Or have I?'

His tone invites no further question. He stands with his back to us, a sombre massive figure like the hill itself, thick grey hair and beard protruding from between cap and collar. She places a fresh basin of hot water at his feet. 'You can wash here in the warm. It must be cold out on the mountains.'

I put the bundle of clean clothes beside the basin and follow her into the kitchen. The two fowl are lying on the table cleaned and plucked, beside them a mound of stuffing like snow on muddy earth.

'When are you leaving?'

'Tomorrow night.'

'You'll see Christmas Day out then?'

'For your sake, yes.'

'For all our sakes. The boy—'

'Is well over the worst. He'll be able to travel. Have no fear for him.' On impulse I cross to a cupboard and take from it a bottle still half filled with whisky. I pour a glass and drink it straight down, the sudden burning sensation bringing a feeling of pleasure. Taking the bottle and a glass I go back to the range and put them on the mantleshelf. 'The season,' I say. But still he stands silently brooding into the fire. I turn and leave.

Outside I check the pistol and slip it into my belt, then

unload the revolver. It's safer with only one, I think. The dog comes at my soft call, rearing up to put his front paws on my chest. I ruffle his ears and muzzle, thankful for an intimacy which demands no explanation and seeks no complication. I check the barns and outhouses, trying to make simple routine take the edge off fears and questions. But the tension doesn't leave me. I climb to the hilltop and watch in turn each slit of light across the valley, and the soft glow which is the village. The sound of church bells is again in the wind. My own home is in darkness. To my mind comes a picture of the lough with the wind building up the waves and my prison as a swaying square of light. That's how it seemed sometimes, as if it and I were suspended on nothing. The picture fades into one of plodding rain-soaked figures in front of me and hills without end. And then I think that perhaps why I now think so much of yesterday is that I'm becoming afraid of trying to see tomorrow. I think of the sergeant and in this barrenness lean towards him in comfort. I know what it is.

Inside the cottage I find him sitting by the range, boots off, in clean clothes, my clothes, his hands gripping a glass of hot whisky. My enemy.

She comes to me. 'Well?'

'Everything's quiet.'

'I thought I heard the bells for Mass.'

'You did.'

'There'll be many there the night.'

As I take the proffered glass of whisky from her I click the latch and call softly to the dog. He comes in and takes his customary corner. 'It's a night for few others to be abroad.'

The sergeant turns towards me, his expression still closed and brooding. 'Tomorrow?'

'We stay here.'

He nods. 'The boy wants to get up.'

'Then let him. He'll recover all the quicker.'

She's about to go to the stairs when my glance stops her. A moment later he rises and disappears and we listen to his feet above us. 'Let him do it,' I say.

He comes back carrying the boy and sets him in a chair by the fire, gently, as though he were his own. The boy responds, smiling at him out of a thin white face. That trust between them which I noticed at the beginning of the trek has grown. I try to hold his eyes but he avoids my gaze and looks slowly round the room, now filling with the rich smell of cooking. The two fowl are ready for the oven, dough ready for the griddle, jams are taken from their hiding-places. The feast is in preparation. She bustles around us in this haven, goes to stir a pot full of thick soup and offers a plateful to the boy. He sups it, and I pass him a small glass of whisky. In twenty-four hours he must be ready. Despite my attempts at keeping them at bay, thoughts of tomorrow break through.

'What happened?'

It's the sergeant who answers. 'You were ill. Fever.'

'It must have been that freezing lough,' I say, attracting his attention. 'And not being able to dry out afterwards.'

'Where are we?'

I pause to see if the sergeant will answer, but he doesn't. 'My home.'

Again he looks slowly around the room and half smiles, as if to say something. But the exertion's too much. Already he's asleep, his head falling forward. The sergeant leans across and I nod, and the boy is carried back upstairs. I regret his going, welcoming this intrusion which was a distraction from other things. The sergeant returns and we sit opposite one another, more alive to our predicament, but silent. I listen to my wife bolting the doors for the night. Then she goes upstairs, pausing for a moment to rest her hand on my shoulder.

The sergeant is first to break the silence. 'Leave the boy here.'

'For what?' I ask, though I'd already thought of it.

'You'll have him die too?'

'No one's said anything about dying yet.'

'You know your cause is already lost.'

I look directly into his eyes, my voice soft. 'My cause is always lost. Yet somehow is always still alive. Is that not so?' As he doesn't answer, I ask, 'And what if I leave him here? He'll be

84

taken back to a cage. And this time for murder.' I pause for a moment. 'Yes. Murder. Because your side will deny that it's war. And not being war, then you're dealing only with gunmen. Criminals. So being a criminal the boy will rot indefinitely in a cage. Or be hanged.'

'Perhaps he won't be caught. Perhaps they won't come.'

His voice is insincere. They'll come, as they always have. How often have I watched them come up the narrow stony roads in their lorries and armoured cars. Outside the cottages they stop, their rifles lining up the occupants. Perhaps he will be one of them. Was one of them. 'How many homes like this have you raided? Didn't you say you were fighting in the south? Was it with the Black-and-Tans?'

'A good many of us resigned because of them.'

'Resigning isn't enough.'

He lifts a newspaper and reads. 'More executions of Republican prisoners. On December 19th, by order of the newly established Free State government, seven Kildare men—'

'I know.'

'So what if you take him with you? To be shot by his own, is it? His own. Does he know who his own are?'

'Do we?'

He frowns into the fire. Somehow I've penetrated his thoughts, upset them. We sit in silence again, a baffled silence where we both want to talk yet are afraid to speak. I pull the turf basket to the range and slowly rake and build up the fire for the night. The dog stirs as I make for the kitchen but I shush him and he lies back. I unfold the blankets she has laid out and bring them back to the range, on the way noticing the clock nearly at one. 'It's Christmas Day.'

His face shows nothing. 'Merry Christmas.'

'It's time we got some rest. Proper rest. The first since—' Quickly I stop.

'I'll sleep here alone. She'll need you.' His voice is softer. 'It might be the last time. Don't you think she knows that?'

It's out before I know it, what I didn't want to say, ask. 'Why do you stay? You're no hostage now.' There's anger in my voice.

85

He stares at me. 'Maybe that's so.'

'Why? Why?'

There's anger in his own voice now. 'Don't you know?'

I go upstairs. The boy is on a mattress on the floor, asleep, though his breathing is irregular. Behind the partition I hear the children talking and laughing softly. There'll be little sleep for them tonight. For a moment fear seeps through me as I stand at the window looking out into the night, but nothing moves. Angry at myself I slip into bed trying not to disturb her, but she responds to my touch and immediately turns into me. I fall asleep and soon am awake again, aware of my own hard flesh and the urgency of her body against mine. In the physical expression of our love there's peace, a moment of true forgetfulness, of innocence almost. Memory is suspended, the past does not exist. Sated, I lie back thinking that this might be a child I shall never see and so in a sense is not mine. It belongs solely to her, to cherish, fuss over, be burdened with. When I wake the second time I am alone. From below, I hear her voice chiding the young ones. The boy is sitting up on the mattress, his back against the partition wall, a blanket around his shoulders. He is watching me, and I get up and go to him.

'How are you feeling?'

'All right now.' He looks around the room and then into my eyes, still unsure of his surroundings. 'Was I bad?'

I nod. 'Very bad.'

'How did I get here?'

'We carried you.'

'We?'

'Me. And the sergeant.'

He speaks as though to himself. 'Yes. The policeman.' He stops, then asks, 'Is he still alive?'

'Yes.'

'Yes. It was the other one. I . . .'

There is innocence in his eyes, in his words too. His voice fades, but still he keeps looking at me, and I think of the other one downstairs, wonder what he's doing, thinking. Hardly the Western Front, he'd said. True. But that kind of war must be

86

easier. Your enemy you can't know. He's not even human, but only a piece of coloured cloth different from yours. But in this kind of war you can know him as you know yourself. It's knowledge like that which brings irresolution.

I pull on some clothes and go to the window, though it's not the hillside I see. On a dawn like this the Republican prisoners file out into the courtyard to face the rifles of those who but a few months ago were their companions. Yes, on this very dawn too, in the gaols and camps of Dublin and the south. Some hesitant, still wanting to live, some uncaring, their lives already ended by a decree that vengeance alone is the rule, as if those now in power had not once fought for independence too. I listen as if it were my own feet I hear shuffling into that yard. To live constantly with defeat, to lose a dream entirely, must be unendurable. For some.

'How far've we got?'

I'm glad at the boy's voice bringing me back to what I should be thinking about. Lighting cigarettes for both of us, I press one into his hand. 'Half-way, roughly. We leave tonight. And we've all day to rest in.' I pause, then say slowly, 'The sergeant says to leave you here.'

'Why?'

'Your strength, for one thing. You must be weak still.' Again I pause. 'And maybe you'd be best out of it.'

'And what'll I do?'

'Stay here. There's nowhere in the six counties you can run to where they won't find you. So stay here till they come for you. You'll be back in prison. But maybe not for long.' I puff at the cigarette, waiting. 'Remember. I forced you to escape. Tell them that.'

'You didn't.'

The simplicity of what he says is painful. Would that all truth were so easy. I study his face. The pallor is going, as are the dark rings from under his eyes. Young and lusty life shakes fever from it as the land shakes off winter. Fresh from this encounter with death, am I to lead him to another?

'I could get a ship.'

'Yes,' I say. 'Leave. Many have had to. And after this, many more will have to.'

'Who's winning?'

'No one.' I try to smile. 'No one can win now.'

'But one side must win.'

I don't answer.

'Yet you'll go on and fight?'

'Yes.'

Her voice calls up the stairs saying that she's leaving for church, that I'm to see to the fowl in the oven. Her words have the easy familiarity of ordinary circumstances, and betray no emotion. In our love in the night she cried. From what? For what? At the window again I pause long enough to watch her walk up the path beyond the outhouses, the young ones around her, and then turn to the boy. 'Try to get up. It's Christmas Day.'

He frowns. 'Christmas? I forgot.'

'It seems we all forgot at some time or other.'

I stop at the foot of the stairs. The sergeant stands in the doorway staring up the hill, and for a moment I try to see into that brooding profile. Part of his thoughts I know. But what of his side in the war? His side that is the main cause of the war yet is not part of it? Between him and the Provisional government in the south the Republic is being crushed, crushed between their implacable wills. And secure in that knowledge it is only then that I realise it's him I no longer want with me, not the boy.

He turns. 'Well?'

'I've told the boy.'

'What?'

'To stay here.'

'And?'

I shake my head. 'Nothing. He said nothing.'

'He's all day to think about it.' He turns away from me once more, looking up the hill.

'Anything about?'

'No.'

88

I join him, clicking my fingers for the dog Shane to come to me. His tongue is warm against my hand. Such life I shall miss. Even this. 'You can too.'

'Can what?'

'Stay.'

'Here?'

I nod. 'Here.'

He faces me again, his expression showing no surprise. 'And you?'

'I'll go on alone.'

'To Donegal?'

'Yes.'

'And as soon as you're over the hill I'll be making for the nearest village to have you stopped before you get there.'

'Will you?' As he doesn't answer, I say, 'They can try. I know this country too well.'

His voice is harsh with decision, as I suspected it would be. 'No. You brought me this far. I'll go the rest.'

'I can make you.'

'Stay?' He shakes his head. 'You can't. What are you going to do? Shoot me?'

It's foolish, what I said. He's right. I see him look past me and then the boy appears beside us.

The sergeant puts his hand on the boy's arm. 'Well, son? Have you decided? You're hardly old enough for wars.'

'I heard you talking,' the boy says, pushing between us and going out into the yard.

By the time she and the young ones return I've repaired the barn door and the others have swept the cottage and yard clean. We all crowd round the fire as the children are given their few presents, items secreted away months before. Maeve is loudest in her chatter and laughter, running from me to the sergeant, ribbons streaming from her doll. I watch him take her in his arms, though his face is still unsmiling. The oldest boy hangs back, no longer a child, not yet a man. I pour whisky for us, giving the oldest boy some from my own glass. It's then she takes me aside.

89

'There's talk of a raid.'

'When?'

'Later today.'

I was wrong. I didn't think they'd come. Quickly I think back over the past few days, wondering what signs we'd left, telling of our direction. Or had the sergeant deliberately marked the path behind us? Doubtful, as he was in my own sight most of the time. 'Where exactly?' I ask.

'Just around. That's all I heard.'

'And if they're just around they've every reason to come here.' I pause. 'We'll go up the hill. And we'll have to take the wee girl.'

'No.'

My voice is sharp. 'We must. She's too young yet. She'll betray us and not even know she's doing it. Be sure they'll ask her.'

'And have them wonder why she's out alone? They know how many of us there are.'

'Sean too,' I say, mentioning the eldest boy. 'She's out with him for a look at the sheep. There's nothing strange about that.'

I collect the guns and ammunition and gather up the police clothes the boy was wearing, tying them into a bundle. The sergeant looks askance at me and I say simply—'Your friends. We're going up the hill a while.' From a hiding-place I take a small pair of field-glasses and go outside to scour the surrounding hills while the others make ready. As we leave I squeeze the other boy's arm, saying nothing. He's seen it before, and knows what to do. Fifty yards behind the barn a gully begins, running up the hill in a jagged crack. We drop into it and make our way to an overhanging cleft near the top. During the climb I remember I meant to tell her about the food. There's so much of it. Too much. But she too has seen it before, many times. Looking back I see the younger boy raking the ground to blur our prints.

'Your line of communications is pretty good.'

It's the sergeant's voice. I acknowledge his humour with a

grin, then take a short piece of rope from my pocket and motion to him to put his hands behind his back.

'Still not trust me?'

'When you're on your own in open country. Not when your friends might be so close you could whisper to them.'

I tie his hands and gag him. The boy is watching us both closely. More than ever he's done before, and I begin to wonder what his decision will be. The sergeant is right. He'll have to decide, and not just be willed by me. As I load and check the rifles I recall our talk of the morning. No one can win now, I'd said. But now my words seem stupid, meaningless. The boy's right. Someone must win.

They come in the heavy light of afternoon. First there is the faint whine of engines and then blobs of light appear over the far hill. I watch through the glasses as the two tenders come down the stony road putting nearby sheep to flight. At the cottage the dog has begun his furious barking, which is briefly drowned as the tenders turn in and sit, engines running. The cottage and barn blocks them from me. Minutes pass before two policemen come in sight round both sides of the house, rifles in hand. The back door opens and she comes out, first going to the door to quieten him. The barking stops and he lies, lolling tongue showing his fangs, the rope at his throat taut where she's tied him to a post.

'What's going on?'

It's the boy's voice. I roll over and hand him the glasses. The wee girl's asleep, wrapped up in Sean's coat and lying at his feet, and I'm thankful, hoping she stays that way.

'The two policemen have gone inside,' the boy says.

I take the glasses again and watch. Though I can see nothing, I know there'll be others round the front.

'What if they come up the hill?'

It's Sean asking. Inside me is that hard knot of rage I haven't felt since escaping from my prison. Rage at this rape of my being. At myself for losing sight of that one single purpose, the trek, for giving way to persuasion, sentiment. In this moment I hate the boy for his illness, his weakness. My own weakness.

Sean's voice again cuts through my thoughts. 'We'll go on,' I say. 'You cut across the hill with Maeve. If they do run across you tell them you've been out with the sheep. But make sure they see you in time. Give them no cause to shoot.'

'And you'll be back?'

'Depends how far they come,' I say, knowing I won't.

'They're outside again,' the boy says.

It's the same two as before. They slowly cross the yard, eyes on the ground. A third joins them. Beyond the edge of the farm buildings they spread out over the grass, each of them stopping now and again to look up the hillside. Others will be doing the same at the front. Even against the chill I feel a slight prickle of sweat on my skin. What if the younger boy has failed to remove all the signs of our presence? And inside? In my mind I see the interior of the cottage. She'll be bustling around, doing things to show that she refuses to allow them to upset her routine, a match for the Inspector in charge, who'll be lounging in a chair while casually talking, probing, trying to corner both her and the boy. Again that anger at myself comes to the surface, this time for not being ready in case such a likelihood happened. Should we be forced to go on, now we've only the guns. No food, dry clothes, any of the other items we need. I pass the glasses back to the boy. 'Keep a sharp eye.'

Sean crosses the gully and stands to look over the top, but I pull him back. My voice is harsher than intended. 'Don't leave the wee one! What if she wakes and starts crying?'

He pulls his arm away from me, sullen rebelliousness on his face. A good sign, I think. Maybe he'll have to learn to think for himself sooner than he wants to. He returns to his former position, his arm lightly across his still sleeping sister. 'What're they doing?'

'Searching outside.' I pause and look at the sergeant. 'I s'pose we could have good information of what's going on if he could talk. He's an old hand at raids, is this one.'

But the sergeant shows no sign of hearing. He sits upright, hands still tied, head lolling forward and with his eyes closed.

Sean nods at him. 'Where'd you capture him?'

'Above Larne. The night of the escape.'

'Ma says there was another one.'

'Maybe,' I say.

His voice is soft, yet anxious. 'I heard her say too the Republic can't win. That you'll only be shot like the others. By the Free Staters.'

'Are you afraid?'

'Afraid of what?'

'Of hearing one day that I've been shot?'

He's silent for a long time. 'Yes.'

I too am silent, then say, 'I would be too. But then I'd have to think that he knew what he was doing even if it happened. And it was for the best.'

He doesn't speak after that, but lies staring at the sky. I too lie down, feeling the earth and the sky pressing against me, making me feel puny. My children are beside me, a boy, an old man who is my enemy. An enemy I won't kill. Can't kill now. And I can offer no protection to any of them.

'They're going.'

As the glasses are pressed into my hand the sudden crackle of engines splits the air apart and echoes in the hills. From the yard the policemen disappear round the side of the cottage. Bands of light cut through the dusk and then the tenders come into sight, square and bulky, moving slowly up the road. I watch, half expecting them to stop again. But no. Their lights vanish over the hilltop, leaving only the faint whine of engines to ruffle the quiet. Then that too fades.

Sean rises. 'Will I go on down?'

'Yes. And take the wee girl. If it's all right, send the dog up. If he doesn't come I'll know something is wrong.'

'And if there is?'

'We'll go on. We can't stay any longer.' I put my hand on his shoulder. 'Take care of the rest.'

Without answering he takes Maeve in his arms and steps out of the gully, walking across the hill before turning down so that he approaches the cottage from a different angle. I squint through the glasses again but darkness is rolling in quickly and it's difficult to see. Perhaps the raid was a good thing. My senses are alert once more and it's as though I feel the force of the land itself press me on, imbued as it is with my bloody ancestry.

I hear the grass rustling, then the dog comes bounding into the hollow and pushes his muzzle against my chest as I take the note tied round his neck by a piece of cord. It simply says they've gone. I nod towards the sergeant and tell the boy to untie him.

'What now?' the boy asks, beginning to unloosen the rope.

'We go back to the cottage. We've about eight hours before we leave.'

The sergeant stands up, chafing his wrists and stamping his feet. 'Who leave? Have you made up your mind yet, son? This isn't your fight.'

My words are out without thinking. 'Not his fight? It belongs to us all. This is what he inherits. What you and I inherit. What my sons inherit. What your sons inherit.'

His voice is intense and savage. 'My sons? My sons? What do you know of my sons?'

'That they'll do as you do. Fight against the country they live in so that they can pay fealty to an English monarch. And what does that make you? In England you're nothing. Of no particular worth. Here you're even less. Fodder for English wars. To maintain an empire of servants by any means at all for their glory.'

'And what do you want me to exchange for that? A Popish empire where I'll even be told how to think? A Popish Republic?'

'Hardly a Popish Republic when it has a Protestant history. A Republic in the spirit of Tone. Joy McCracken.'

'Aye. I can just see it. A Free-thinking Republic as dictated by the Catholic church. Are you mad enough to think that after all these centuries the church is going to hand its power over to you?' Suddenly he turns to the boy, his voice still savage. 'There you are, son. A simple choice. Choose. Here in the north we've no friends. Only those who want to use us. Fight for England. A country that'll keep you poor for its own glory and sell you down the river if need be. Or a Republic that'll keep you poor for the glory of the Holy Christian Empire as ruled by the Roman administrator Paul. You've a choice of devils. We must be the only people on earth who kill each other for the privilege of saying which devil we run with.'

But before the sergeant has finished the boy has already turned away and started to clamber down the gully. For a few moments we stand looking after the retreating figure and then the sergeant begins to laugh loudly, abruptly, that same laughter I heard when I'd returned after inspecting the dugout, mocking, as if in condemnation of us both, when he'd said something about God being funny. I wondered afterwards what he meant. The laughter doesn't stop, but increases, booming out, bursting into my head, and I hear myself shouting Shut up! Shut up! without being aware of speaking, aware only of my newly wakened resolve weakening in the face of this onslaught and the boy's sudden going. Calling the dog I sling the rifles over my shoulder and follow him, pausing near the foot to look back. The sergeant's bulk is lost in the night. There's only the sound, not so loud now, a laughter which has no trace of humour. The only note I can pick out is one of pain, a sound like that from some wounded thing which rouses me from sleep to lie wondering at its origin, a sound of desolation from some brute beast trying to give voice to an instinct even it doesn't understand.

The table is partly laid when I arrive at the cottage. I put the guns out of sight and with some ceremony pour glasses of lemonade for the wee girl and whisky for the rest, but she insists on whisky too and we make some merriment of that as I give her a small glass. She begins to sing a carol, her voice clear and pure, unafraid of her listeners. I watch this dark-haired, dark-eyed child, seeing her as a young woman crossing the hillside, the natural grace of her body and uplifted breast like the fern running and dipping in the summer wind. Just as I first saw her, she from whose womb this child came. My child, my daughter. Lying on the hill where I'd fallen after a boisterous night on the poteen. As I struggled out of sleep she was a vision as she crossed

95

the fields to the village and I lay with that savage tender knot in my belly that told me this was her I wanted, wanted to know, would never know. Would never know her fully for somewhere in her lay a part beyond my taking. Buried deep and blind in the dark mass of her thighs as her body saps my strength in that moment of nothingness that is like death. My child.

I go to her in the kitchen where she's arranging plates, standing behind her to cross my arms over her breasts, kissing the grey strands of her dark hair. 'Well?'

'We're ready to eat.'

I turn her round. Her eyes are filmed over, giving nothing, hiding herself and her fear within herself. For a moment she leans her forehead against my shoulder. But there can be no comfort now. I return to the other room to refill my glass. The girl's still singing. The younger boy sits beside her, chin in cupped hands, listening. A solitary one, that one, who'd rather talk to himself. Born of the land, yet he doesn't belong to it. Perhaps one for the priesthood. The other two sit talking quietly and as I look at the boy who is my companion it's as though I've been graced with another son.

I go to the kitchen again. Her face is calm but still her eyes give little. 'What happened?'

'They just stayed awhile. Looked around.'

'I watched them from the hill. Poking around outside. Did they ask much?'

'The Inspector mostly just sat. Said there'd been no sign of you since the escape. Asked if I knew where you'd go. I told him you kept those things to yourself. And he asked about the children.'

'You told him they were out with the sheep?'

'Yes. And then he said wasn't I afraid for the wee one, letting her out in the hills in winter? But I told him that was a stupid thing to say because didn't she have to get to know the hills like anybody else and wasn't the older boy with her to teach her to know them? It would be a bad thing growing up and not knowing them.'

'And that's all? They stayed long enough.'

'He just sat by the fire and looked, mostly. As I went about doing whatever I had to do. I wasn't going to stop for him. As I told him.'

As I knew it would be as I lay back up there on the hill. But an hour before he sat by my fire. My enemy. Silently looking into every corner. Sitting, cap on his knees, hands outstretched to the flames probably. At home. Yet waiting ready with some simple everyday word and watching for her to betray herself.

'He even looked in the oven.'

Unease comes. 'And saw two fowl? Two fowl for a woman and children?'

It is the first time I've seen her smile since coming back. 'There was only one. The other was well out of sight.'

But the unease doesn't leave me. What else might those sharp eyes have seen? 'Did he question the boy?'

'Who didn't answer him.'

I smile too, trying to make light of it. 'A non-talker that one, for sure. He doesn't even talk to me.' I pause, wanting to know her own instincts. 'And what do you think?'

'On the way out he said he didn't really think you'd make this way anyway.' She too pauses, then says, 'They won't be back. Not for a while. I think he believes what he says.' She lifts her glass and drinks. 'He seemed a decent man. Like that one you brought with you.'

I kiss her. 'That's true of most of us,' I say, feeling her tremble slightly in my arms. The raid has upset her more than I thought.

'What will happen?'

'I know the future no more than you. All I know is I must go to Donegal.'

'Must?'

'Must,' I say quickly, allowing her no indication of doubt.

The girl's voice falls silent. She breaks away from me. 'Eat. At least we're alive to eat a Christmas dinner, thank God.' She leaves me and I hear her rattling the pots on the range as I finish my whisky, pushing all other thoughts from my mind save the

97

sergeant. She comes in again. 'The plates are warming up. Where's the other one?'

'I was just thinking about him,' I say, going to the door. He stands in the barn, motionless like a carved figure. 'You must be cold,' I say.

'Aye. Cold as the grave itself.'

'Come in. We're ready to eat.'

He stands for a while, ignoring me. As he turns and passes by me, I notice his face and hands are streaked black as though he had been digging in the earth. I follow him, pausing as he turns into the kitchen to splash water on his face, then go to the range to rake the fire into a bright glow which spills across the room. Fully laid now, the table is pulled into the centre. I motion the children and the boy to their places, reserving the chair with its back to the fire for her and the one beside it for the sergeant. He comes in, face impassive, as she ladles potatoes and vegetables onto the plates, and empties his glass in one swift movement. I carve and share the pieces among the plates. Broken only by the scrape of knives, the silence becomes oppressive. Gently I stroke my daughter's hair, asking her to sing, and she does so as before, without shyness, her high child's voice unfaltering. All our eyes are on her until suddenly a second voice breaks in, the sergeant's, soft and deep, the two voices mingling under the low beamed ceiling. Finishing, she impulsively jumps up to put her arms round him, kissing his bearded cheek, and we watch as he breaks off a sprig of holly from the branch tied to the beams and weaves it into her dark hair, the bright berries glinting in the glow of the lamp, as the rest of us clap our hands.

Indicating the plate with the other fowl, I say, 'You carve.'

He hesitates a moment, then begins to cut, distributing the slices around the table.

'Where's your house?' It's the girl speaking, her curiosity at last finding utterance.

Quickly the sergeant looks at her. 'House?'

'Your own house. Why are you here with us?'

My own voice is sharp. 'Enough.' Then I add, 'Sing to us some more.'

98

But she hurries on, pretending she hasn't heard me. 'Who'll do the carving in your house? With you not at home?' The last question fades into a whisper as she timidly looks round the table, fear creeping into her face at the feeling of tension now so suddenly part of the scene.

Rising, my wife brushes past the sergeant and puts her arms round her shoulders. 'That's enough, Maeve. You were told. Sing to us again. Like you did.'

'My home?'

The sergeant is staring straight ahead, his face creased and eyes almost closed, veins ridged on his temples and forehead, as if caught in a trance never to move again. His hands lie on the table at either side of the plate, thick heavy fingers white with the intensity of his grip on carver and fork.

I know, I know what it is, and under my breath beg him don't, don't.

'I was only—' The wee girl breaks off, burying her head in her mother's lap as she begins to cry. In the sergeant's eyes there are tears also. His voice, though as soft as a woman's, falls against my ears as savage as the elements.

'That was my son you killed back there on Slemish. My only son.'

It isn't the fear that holds me, but that paralysis when a man can no longer run but must turn and face the tempest at his back.

'My son. My only begotten son. Trussed and his neck wrung as if no more than this chicken we eat. Lying back there on Slemish. Rotting under a pile of stones with not even a shroud to cover him. Your work!'

I try to reach the pistol as his bulk crashes the table against me. But nothing can withstand this fury.

Shaking my head to clear the red dim mist from my sight I become aware that someone is bathing my face. She kneels beside me with a cloth and a basin of pink coloured water. The table lies on its side amid broken plates and scattered morsels of food. Opposite me is the eldest boy, arms around the wee girl, whose face is buried in his chest. The other boy is standing at the range, his collar grasped in the sergeant's left hand, the other hand holding the pistol to his temple. Standing beside me also is the other boy, my companion, his gaze moving from the sergeant to me, face showing nothing. As I slowly take in the details the clogging in my ears lessens too and there comes the sound of crying. It is the girl.

'Tidg.'

'I can see now,' I say, taking her hand where she is still kneeling beside me.

The sergeant holds the boy out from him, the pistol now a little way from his head. 'Can you see?'

I nod. 'Yes.' The boy shows no sign of fear, but simply looks at me.

'My only son,' the sergeant says.

'And I have two.'

I can feel her body beside me beginning to convulse and I am standing helpless by the bed watching her labour in birth, her voice a whisper, 'No, Tidg, no.'

My voice still sounds as though it comes from some place far away from me. 'One of the many stories I've read. This one of the '98 rebellion. Here in the north. A woman was asked to choose which of her sons was to be hanged. The eldest or the youngest.'

His face is still creased with pain. 'And which did she choose?'

'Neither. And that choice drove her insane too. As any other would have done.'

'And which did they choose?'

'The youngest. And then they forced the eldest boy to be executioner.'

'And him?'

'He hanged himself.'

'They?'

'The militia men.'

'Militia?'

'You.'

'Me.'

It is not a question.

The girl lifts her face up to him. 'Where is your house?'

His voice is soft. 'By their fruits ye shall know them.'

Beside me her body still convulses, and I grip her hard to prevent her from moving.

The pistol spins in the air and clatters across the stone flags of the floor. 'Vengeance is not mine, said my God. I can't speak for yours.' Quickly he passes us and I can hear the door closing.

Painfully I get to my feet, but now it is her wrath which breaks and she is hitting me across the face and chest with her fists, her cry a lamentation. 'His only son? His only son? No, Tidg, no. No no no no no no no no.'

Gently I force her into a chair and turn to my sons. 'See to the house.' The boy is still watching me. 'And you? You'll stay now?'

'No. I'll go with you.' He pauses. 'And with him.'

'Then get the clothes and food. I'll get the guns.' After collecting the weapons I pull on a hunting coat and begin to thrust whisky and other articles into the deep pockets. Then I toss one of the greatcoats to the boy, and, taking the other, go outside, where I find him standing in the yard. 'Here,' I say, putting it across his shoulders.

'The boy?'

'Means to go.'

'And you'll let him? Even now?'

'It's his choice.' I pause. 'As it's yours. Has been.' The dog Shane comes over to me, thrusting his head against my thigh. 'Well?'

'I violated your home. That I didn't mean.'

My eyes hold his, my tone is matching his, my hand almost touching his. 'You violated my home? What have I done to yours?'

The boy leaves the cottage and crosses the yard towards us, a sack over his shoulders.

The sergeant turns to him. 'You won't stay?'

'What for?'

Behind the anguish of the sergeant's face I can see a smile. 'What does a dolphin mean to you, son?'

'A free thing. A girl.'

My voice is harsh again as I ask the sergeant. 'Well?' Getting no answer I turn to the boy. 'Tie the dog up. He's needed here.'

Re-entering the cottage, I find her sitting in a chair, the girl trying to comfort her. I kneel and put my arms round them both, feeling their warmth flow into my body. Then I hold each of the boys tightly against me. There is nothing to say, nothing that can be said. Outside the sergeant is ready, his coat buttoned against the rising wind, the sack across his shoulder which he has taken from the boy. There's a kind of fury inside me as I shout, 'Why do you come? Why? Why?'

'To watch you die by your own kind.'

'Are you not my kind also?'

'To watch you die,' he says again, then passes me and follows the boy, whose vague outline I see already moving up the hillside. Before moving after him I pause to ruffle the dog's head and ears and slip my fingers through his jaws, listening to the low whine whose cause will soon be forgotten. How envious one can be of a beast of the field.

Half-way up the slope the indistinct but certain sound of gunfire reaches us from some far hillside, and as I try to seek out my home in the dark valley below and still sense Shane's dark muzzle on my thigh and become aware of him I violated watching me intently, it's as though drifting towards me are those faint sounds inexorably and unmistakably pealing out my own doom.

Five

Now there was frost in the hills, and at times soft flurries of snow broke and melted across their faces, stinging, momentarily blinding them. Higher up, the earlier snow and rain had frozen hard and impeded fast going, making them slither and stumble. The Sperrins lay all around them in patches of glistening white and long stretches of pitted terrain where the gorse had become knotted with the wind and now pulled at their feet. The taller peaks seemed sometimes to float among the clouds and press down on them from a jagged sky, in their vastness dwarfing them and making them feel insignificant.

It was the boy who felt this most. His returning strength brought a state of heightened yet confused perception which made him feel that he was witnessing this mountain landscape as a living breathing thing. Each blade of grass was a multitude of mottled writhing blobs held together in a pale shimmer of green, the ridges circles of bright darkness ringed through each other. And it was the mountains that seemed to move, cutting across his vision in a criss-cross pattern of lines, both stark and smudged. It was as if they were being tested, their strength, endurance. Before being judged.

'How's the going?'

It was the sergeant behind him, his beard glistening, one hand reaching out to touch his shoulder. It was a gesture of comfort the boy wanted to accept, but didn't, and simply nodded his head before moving on. But there was another feeling at work, a sense of wanting in some way to reciprocate this tenderness. The beard and bushy eyebrows reminded him of his own father. As a boy of ten he'd watched him leave the cottage in the glens, kitbag on his shoulder, seaman's cap at a jaunty angle. The ship, a big schooner, was leaving Belfast, bound for South America. On other voyages he'd saved enough money to buy the land and begin the sheep herd. But this ship didn't come back. Then his older brother took over the land and he himself had gone to sea at thirteen. It was always that way, simply because there wasn't enough land. And during the six years he'd spent at sea, of all the songs and shanties he'd learned, it was the ones about the cape of storms that made his eyes wet with emotion. Except for that one other. That morning was like a dream, awakening one morning in a Chinese port in the arms of a dark-haired slit-eyed girl whose skin was like gold. Before, he'd known only the beauty and savagery of the sea. But now, at sea again, he began to know its loneliness. A bit like the loneliness of the mountains. Love is kind. Love is kind to the least of men.

It was the girl singing in the cottage that had brought all those scenes tumbling into his mind. The woman too. The girl unformed. Long-legged like a bird in the shingle. The woman solid, heavy-breasted. Bustling about with her long skirt swinging. Leaning over the range with the fire making her bare arms shine. The thoughts came then in unruly clamour. Of money spinning across bartops and women spinning in the smoky air. The colourful crowded streets. The warmth of her bed. And the memory of it during the long arduous hours on board when the only comfort was a brief rest, sitting alone watching the sea's black immensity and the sun a fuzzy blob rising swiftly from its depths like a dolphin with the moon and stars on its back. Love is kind.

Yes. He had been going to sing. He could still hear the unfaltering sound of the girl's voice. And then the sergeant's chiming in, wavering, breaking. He was going to sing the song he loved, the song he instinctively knew that touched more than himself, that lay in the blood of generations of seafaring men.

And then it had happened, with the sergeant lunging across the table at the man like a shaggy bear, his head butting the other on the forehead, hands wresting the half-drawn pistol from his grip. He'd stood there doing nothing, just watching as Sean, the eldest son he'd been talking to, tried to hit the sergeant and was tossed aside. And then the gun being put to the other boy's head and the sergeant saying to the woman—Wake him up! Wake him up! And the woman then getting the basin of water, saying nothing.

My son, the sergeant had said. My only son. He still remembered it vividly, in detail, the swiftness of it, the savagery. And yet so easily done. It was the first time he'd seen someone killed. The wire round his throat and the next moment he was dead. Dead still trying to untie his bootlaces. Ned. And then he recalled how he'd thought earlier that somehow Ned was with them. He felt it even more strongly now. It was strange to think that way, yet it was true. And despite the remembered detail, he wondered if he'd taken it in properly. It had startled him, even sickened him like the first few times he'd ripped the bellies of fish, but was so different. He'd just been another policeman, one of those he'd learned to fear. A uniform makes a man look different.

Naked he lay with the white skin showing through the bits of branches and the sergeant saying, No No No, I won't move till he gets a decent grave. His father. Should have known then. My son. My father. Can't say that now.

And the sergeant with the gun to the other one's head. His son. What if he'd pulled the trigger?

And the story too. What if they made you hang your own brother? Or shoot him?

A feeling like no other feeling he'd ever known began to pervade his senses. Not fear. He'd known that at sea when the gales must surely swamp the ship and take her down with all hands. The enormity of each wave carrying them dizzily into a trough with the timbers groaning meant that their frailty would never rise again. Neither ship nor man. But that you learned to know. And learned to know your fear too. It was a different feeling now, a not knowing that was deeper than fear. Despair. And only now did he understand the man's stories about reprisals, about Republican prisoners being taken out of their cells and shot. He could feel it inside him as though it were himself. Filing out into the grey dawn. This dawn. He swung the rifle from one shoulder to the other and back again. Before it had not been part of him. Now it was between him and death.

Another snow shower fell against his face, briefly blinding him. It came with a gust of wind, the flakes sticking to his eyelids before trickling down his cheeks like tears, pricking his eyes like the salt in spray. Turning his head out of the wind to wipe his face he saw the sergeant some dozen yards behind. Head bent into the collar of the greatcoat, peak of the cap pulled across his forehead, hands swinging loosely at his sides with the sack of provisions in one, he was like some shaggy beast in a storybook stumbling to its winter home, and again the boy thought of a bear. He paused, the feeling still inside him of wanting to touch, then turned again, uncertain, beginning to walk quickly, feet sliding and knocking on stones, trying to catch up with the man in front, who had disappeared into the swirling flakes which now blotted out the peaks and marooned them on a tiny patch of mountain earth.

The feelings he had about the two men were at odds with the way he should have been feeling. He saw himself lying on the grass with the sergeant showing him how to be accurate with a gun when they'd shot the hare for something to eat. And how he'd thrown the pistol away. Vengeance is not mine, he'd said. The other one was so unlike him, always cold, shut in, silent, driving on.

Yet he'd been given the choice to stay. The cottage would be a warm, comfortable place, somewhere to hide and think for a while. But now he would have to do his thinking in the mountains with that moment when he would have to fight drawing closer. And he didn't even know the reason for his choice. Perhaps it was like that bit in the man's story. Not to choose is a choice too. Suddenly he felt tired.

The figure of the man broke through the snow. He was crouching, rifle across his knees, head aslant into the wind. The boy stopped beside him and leaned against a rock. The sergeant joined them and crouched also, peering into the darkness.

For a moment the boy listened, wondering. 'What is it?'

The man didn't move. With the snow and patches of dark clothes he seemed part of the mountain itself. 'Gunfire.'

Turning his head into the wind the boy listened. But only once did he hear a soft popping sound that reminded him of a cork being pulled.

The sergeant turned his head slightly, concentrating. 'Where do you reckon?'

'North-west,' the man said.

'How far?'

'Can't tell in this weather. Can't even tell whether it's rifles or if they've started shelling again.' He paused. 'Can you?'

The sergeant's tone was mocking. 'D'you want me to change sides as well?'

'I only thought with you in the trenches—'

'Aye. That I'd know better than you. I told you. All I want is to see you die. And maybe them's the guns that'll do it.'

Still they crouched, listening, their bodies in the same posture and almost touching. And as the boy watched them it was as though, with the snow still flurrying round them, the two figures had merged into one.

The sergeant was the first to stand up. 'Where are we?'

'South of Gortin. Mullaghearn mountain.'

'Near Omagh then.'

'Aye. One of your garrisons. But the shooting's hardly coming from there.'

The boy turned his ear into the wind again, but still heard nothing. Softly the sergeant spoke. 'It's not shelling.' He paused. 'But we don't know which side it's coming from. Yours. Mine. Or the others.' He paused again. 'The others. The Free Staters. The ones that are winning the war. Your war.'

The man's voice too was soft. 'If it's not your war as well, why're you still dying?'

The snow had stopped suddenly, making the mountains loom larger than before, the small group of figures now seemingly lifeless and at one with the rocks.

The sergeant turned and leaned beside the boy, his eyes still on the crouching form. 'How far's the border?'

'You made it. Why do you have to ask me?' The man was silent for a moment. 'And it seems those that made it still don't know where it is. Or how far it extends.'

The sergeant moved closer to the boy, turning slightly to look into his face, suddenly aware that the latter hadn't spoken throughout the climb since leaving the cottage. But all the other's countenance showed was a blank stubbornness, before he quickly averted his gaze. And then the incongruity of the man's statement forced its way into the sergeant's mind and he wanted to laugh, though laugh in the same crazy fashion as earlier. The man spoke true. He had no making in the border. That was mainly why he was fighting. That Ireland, Ulster, was now divided for the first time in history. And true that no one was quite sure just where the border lay in places, or how long it would last in its present form. Briefly he thought of Belleek, with the village suffering an invasion of British soldiery and the newly formed RUC. The shelling over the low thatched roofs at the hidden positions of the Republicans with their rifles and machine-guns trying to cut out the western enclave of the new northern State. He had been one of them, drafted from the violent streets of Belfast.

Slowly the man stood up, fingers kneading the joints of his legs. 'It's quiet.'

'So?'

'We're too far from the border so it's hardly Free Staters. Maybe Republican troops have come over.'

'And it's hardly that before they've finished the fight on their own territory.'

'And so it can only be some of my own boys of one of the Northern Divisions.' The man paused. 'And the police.'

The sergeant stretched and moved away from the rock. Of course. It hadn't occurred to him before to think of what command the man belonged to. 'And what rank are you?'

'Brigade Commandant.'

The sergeant tossed the sack across his shoulder. 'What now?' Pausing, he watched the other turn his head this way and that. But now there was a sense of uncertainty about this once implacable presence. Then he added, 'Commandant?'

'We hole up.'

He couldn't curtail the mocking tone. 'So soon again? After only a bout of rifle-fire?'

The man pointed to the boy still resting against the rock, the thin pale face clearly showing fatigue, the former's voice refusing to acknowledge the sergeant's challenge. 'There's him you're so worried about. And the going's bad.' Taking the rifle from the boy and carrying it and his own in the crook of his left arm, he turned and began climbing again, in a few moments becoming lost from sight.

The sergeant turned to the boy. 'Come on. Only he knows these mountains and God knows where we are.'

'Is he doing it for me?'

'Doing?'

'Holing up again.'

Holding out his hand as the boy pushed himself up from the rock, the sergeant noticed how weak the other was. But his assistance was ignored as the boy moved away, then paused to look up towards where the man had disappeared.

'Well? Is it?'

'Why, son?'

'Because I'd rather stay here. Go back. Than stop him. Slow him down. Make him . . .'

The voice trailed off, faltering, wavering, groping for new words as the boy struggled with a new knowledge of self. And as he listened the sergeant felt his own senses falter as new knowledge became his too. He was losing the boy. Losing him at the exact moment when he began to understand that he'd been trying to win him. Not win him over to any cause. Not necessarily that. Win his respect. Win the boy's love. Caught up in the stubborn enmity and bitterness between himself and the man was an unspoken contest about the boy.

Again the boy asked, 'Well?'

'No. There's more in his mind than us. If it was just a matter of slowing him down he'd simply dump us here and go on alone. He's like that.'

The boy nodded. 'Yes. That's the way I saw him on the prison-ship. Hard like that.' Pausing, he added, 'But just then I wasn't sure if that's the way I saw him any more.'

Turning, the boy started to clamber upwards, slowly, painfully, the sergeant behind him following his progress and ready should he fall, thinking that the boy too had sensed something about the man, had seen some crack in that inviolate will gradually opening like a cleft in the rocks, and wondered.

He loomed out of the snow above them, straight-backed, both rifles now over one shoulder, his heavy jacket lying open as though contemptuous of the cold. Reaching down he grasped the boy with one hand and lifted him effortlessly onto the ridge beside him, then reached down again to help the sergeant and, as the latter felt the strong grip pulling him slithering upwards, it suddenly came to his mind that this was the first time their hands had touched.

Kneeling on the ridge, the sergeant began rubbing the numbness from his hands and fingers. 'How far? The boy's done on his feet.'

The man pointed towards a fissure in a sheer face of rock. 'We're here.' Then, lifting the sack the sergeant had been carrying, he said, 'Bring the boy.'

It was a cave this time. A narrow rocky passage ran some dozen yards then abruptly stopped at a large boulder. Putting his shoulder to it the man pushed, and in the heavy light the sergeant saw it move easily aside, as if hinged, showing a dark opening roughly waist high and the same in breadth. As the man bent down a darkish red form leapt furiously out and hit the man's shoulder, sending him reeling, and then the sergeant's thigh before vanishing down the passage.

Exclaiming, the sergeant spun round. 'What the hell!'

A long, low laugh came from the figure on the ground. 'Fox.

Thought he'd make this his lair, eh? Stupid of me. I should've smelt him.'

The sergeant reached out for the boy, now resting against the boulder, his senses still keen to the man's mood, aware that this was the first time he'd heard him laugh, and a laugh of simple pleasure.

Like the dugout, the cave was clean, dry, and not badly stocked. Within a few minutes an oil lamp flickered in a corner, throwing out a circle of yellow light. The cave itself was quite large, the sergeant noticed, large enough to hold a dozen men in comfort. And with being in the fissure, almost impossible for someone to find. The only discomfort was that, for tall men like them both, it was only shoulder high. He watched the man sniffing, poking a stick into the dark corners, as he too began to smell the stench of fox, and heard the man laugh again.

'Hasn't been long here. Just nosing. Still too much human smell about for him to make what he wants of it.'

'Better than we had. Rats are worse. A damn sight worse.'

There was a pause. 'Aye. I forgot. The trenches.'

'And this is better than anything we ever had. Knee deep in every kind of stink. Human flesh and all.' The sergeant paused. 'No wonder you've managed to keep going so long. With most things against you.'

It was a salute. A salute to the endurance and skill of your enemy. He hadn't meant to say it. But now it was out. And in the semi-darkness he saw the man look at him intently for a moment, recognising it for what it was, though passing over it in silence.

Swiftly the man made up a blanket bed in the corner. 'The boy?'

'Already asleep.'

'Bring him over.'

After rolling the boy up, the man tossed blankets to the sergeant. Rummaging in the sack, he pulled out the remains of a bottle of whisky and passed it across. Silently the two drank, the bottle going to and fro between them until it was empty, the man then turning over to blow out the lamp. 'Rest now,' he said. 'Sleep.'

It was a long day and night. And another day. And another night. Time passed, yet did not pass. In the day, there was the gloom of the cave. In the night too. The daylight was like the lamp. With the sun up, a pale yellow glow. Even when it wasn't up, somehow there was still a pale yellow glow. Or so it seemed to the sergeant. Several times he said to the man—A good place, this. Better than the trenches. But all the other did was to look up and watch him silently. Only once did he say something, and that was—The fox. He won't be back. A good beast the fox is.

He's a man from the mountains, the sergeant thought. This is his home. Like the fox. Bending, going out along the rocky passage to wash in the snow and frost-bound grass and heather he carried with him the set features of the man, expressionless again, like the rock on the cliff face. The crack had been covered over. But the sergeant was waiting till it showed again.

The boy slept. When he twisted and turned they both carried him out to piss and shit in the snow and the frost, and carried him back again. It became a ritual. A ceremony. In between times they pushed hot food down his throat.

What are you thinking, the sergeant asked continually. And continually watched.

The face of the man was like a dead thing as he sat against the wall of the cave. Eyes turned inwards, mouth drawn tightly, he was like the land itself in its sombre winter habit.

It was a long day and night. And another day. And another night. Time passed, yet did not pass. In the evening and the morning and the evening there was always the peculiar light of the mountains.

My son is dead, the sergeant said. On Slemish. On the mountains. On the mountains of Ulster. And then, watching the man and the boy, said also, As we are.

When will we waken, the sergeant said, watching the dead face of his living enemy.

It was the third day when the man began to make his preparations. In the morning he left the cave for about an hour, taking the guns and field-glasses. The sergeant sat a little way from the passage, watching the boy walking round and round flexing his muscles and stretching, noting the latter's full recovery after more than forty-eight hours' sleep and wondering about the man and the long delay. The weather had become milder, and now and then the shifting cloudbanks parted and weak sunlight splashed across their faces and brought into prominence the sharper contours of the mountains. It felt good.

When the man returned he carried only the glasses. The sergeant immediately noticed the absence of the guns, and wondered again, noticing also that without them the man's stature did not diminish. He remained a fighter, force and determination showing in every line of his body. Twice during the next few hours the sergeant spoke to him, but was greeted with silence as before. The other sat several yards away, both hands holding the glasses as he studied the landscape. It was around mid-afternoon, when daylight began to fail, that he abruptly stood up and went into the cave, as though some decision had been reached. The sergeant waited till the boy had followed him, then followed in his turn.

Inside the cave the man had lit the small stove and was heating the gruel that had been their diet for three days. They had just kept adding whatever they had to it, barley, potatoes, chicken bones.

'Well?' the sergeant said. 'Why the delay?'

'I have to know,' the man said without looking up and speaking as though to himself, 'what's happening on the border. The best way to get across it. What's happening with the war.' He paused to pour some of the gruel into a can, then chewed slowly. 'I have to know where the soldiers on this side are concentrated most. And where's best on the other side to join up with Republican troops. Which way to go. Either north into Donegal or south into Sligo.'

The sergeant took a can of gruel the boy had poured out for him. 'And how do you propose to find out?'

'I'm going into town.'

The boy looked at him quickly. 'The garrison town?'

There was a smile on the man's face, the sergeant noticed. 'They'll hardly expect me to turn up there.'

Momentarily the sergeant thought of Omagh and the extensive military barracks housing various units of the British army. The streets would be filled with soldiers and police, checking and double-checking to guard against a sudden guerrilla attack. It would bode no good for the newly created northern State if the Republicans could manage to hit an important military base well inside its own territory. It was a possibility, even though they were fighting for their existence in a civil war, as their proven tactical skill in the earlier guerrilla war against the British showed. As he watched the man eat he could not deny a feeling of admiration. 'And us? What about us?'

'I don't want to be captured on this side of the border,' the man said. 'Or die either.' And again it was as though he was speaking to himself.

'And us?' the sergeant repeated.

'Stay here.'

'And if you don't come back?'

The man was silent for a long time. 'You're in charge.' He turned to look directly at the sergeant, smiling slowly, speaking very softly. 'You're in charge. My enemy.'

'And if you do? When do we expect you?'

'Tomorrow night. No later.'

'The guns,' the boy said, speaking for the first time. 'Where're the guns?'

'Dumped,' the man said. 'For the moment.'

'I'll need them,' the boy said. 'If you don't come back I'll go on without you.'

The man kept shaking his head from side to side for a long moment, looking both at the boy and the sergeant, then abruptly stood up, head bent under the ceiling of the cave. 'I'll take only these,' he said, lifting the field-glasses, then vanished through the dark opening.

The sergeant waited for a few minutes then walked along the passageway until he was well clear of the fissure, thinking that if there was any time in which to break free, now was the time, yet knowing also that he wouldn't, that the inexplicable bond forged during the trek and which now held them together acted upon them both like a kind of fatalism. He stood for a lengthy while, turning his own words over and over in his mind, attempting to mine their truth—I want to watch you die by your own kind—eyes searching here and there for a figure whom the mountain darkness had already embraced and hidden.

He sat for a while beside the cache where that morning he'd put the guns, listening intently to night sounds, but hearing nothing which could give cause for concern. Opening it, he felt in the darkness and took out a piece of cloth in which he carefully wrapped the glasses. His movements were slow, methodical. Placing them inside he sealed the cache up again. Earlier when he'd opened it he thought he might find news. But there was no information of any kind. At such a time he would have expected at least some message from whoever had been there prior to himself. But it was obvious that this particular one hadn't been opened for some considerable time. His eyes lingered on the collection of arms, seeking some sign. Each lay neatly wrapped, specks of oil glinting in the light. He'd wrapped all four guns he carried, and stacked the ammunition in a box. Unused, they seemed to have an air of purity about them, arms that the war had passed by. Unlike himself. Nor would they be used, except by himself. He had that feeling about them. Despite the gunfire he'd heard a few days ago, he doubted if there was much activity in this part of the country now, those Republicans truly dedicated to the cause having probably gone over the border months before to join their comrades.

Again he paused, wondering whether he should take a pistol. But he'd already decided against that. It had always been his rule not to carry arms of any kind when engaged on a mission such as this one he was now on. Without a gun you could always bluff, cajole, laugh, talk your way out of a difficult situation. With a gun you were immediately known, and immediately lost.

He was annoyed at his own hesitation. That had been his rule also, never to revoke a decision unless absolutely necessary. Lingering on past decisions was a certain way to foul present and future action. Yet now he found himself breaking that rule, and in a kind of baffled anger because he didn't understand why. With his boots he brushed the pebbly ground in the immediate vicinity of the cache, then broke into a steady walk travelling south, every so often stopping to kneel and listen, his shape in the blackness like some nocturnal creature intent only on food and survival.

It was a good two hours before the lights of the town showed ahead of him. He paused on the outskirts, much longer this time. From some distance away he could hear muffled voices and the sound of an engine, which could only mean soldiers or police as there would be a curfew on. There'd be patrols all round the town, of that he felt sure. Retreating about a mile, he skirted the town in a long curve until he was on the south side, then began to approach again, penetrating to the point where he found the railway track, which he followed for a little while before climbing over an embankment. On the other side was a row of small dark houses with enclosed yards. Reaching one, he put his shoulder firmly against the yard door and felt it yield with a scraping sound. Open as always. On the other side he pushed the door tightly shut again, then rolled the large boulder against it, the latter making it appear securely barred for all but those who knew.

Again he paused. She would have heard the scraping, and would be waiting, listening. Three times he tapped lightly on the small window of the scullery door, then spoke softly, hearing the bolt being withdrawn on the other side.

A lamp shone brightly in the kitchen, suffusing the room with a warm glow, and the fire was carefully banked up. The window was draped with a heavy blanket, sealing in the light. The furniture was sparse, and on one wall a few photographs hung, the room itself giving the impression of neatness and order.

'Hungry?' Her finger pointed to where a pot simmered.

'Ready as ever.'

He smiled. 'But first.'

They clung together in their embrace, a display of deep mutual tenderness and love. Their features resembled one another with the high sweeping forehead and prominent cheekbones which cut sharply inwards to a straight even mouth, features which showed a natural dignity. Hers was the younger face, though, where the man's hair showed no trace of grey, hers was totally white except for a black streak on one side which seemed to sharpen the contours of her face.

'Tidg.'

'Cath. Cath.'

'You're cold.'

'Oh, you know I don't feel it. I'm too much part of the mountains for that.'

It was a ritual, this greeting. After a while she pulled away. Silently he watched her every movement as she poured a glass of whisky and held it out to him. He drank it straight down and held it out again as she poured another measure and, this time, one for herself, saluting each other as they sipped.

'Has anyone else been?'

'Not for two weeks. Brennan was the last. The police were on to him.'

'And?'

'He stayed about three days. Then left to try to get across the border.'

He sat down, gazing into the fire. He was right, there wasn't much activity. Momentarily he visualised the small wiry figure of Brennan, trekking alone across the country, and found it comforting, as though he had already made contact. It was the first tangible evidence of others of his cause.

'And you?' she asked.

'We've been holing up in a cave since Monday. It's about ten miles north.'

'Christmas Day.'

He nodded. 'We left around midnight.'

'Left?'

'Home. Maeve.'

'We?'

'A boy. And a policeman. A hostage.' He paused. 'Though hardly a hostage now.'

'Why?'

'I don't quite know.'

'Tell me. Tell me since the escape.'

'You heard?'

'Yes. I heard. But only of the escape. Nothing after that.' She paused, then said again, 'Tell me.'

Only to her had he patiently answered questions. It had been like that even when they were children together. Something in his nature made him instinctively bend to the insistent queries of the rag-tail high-spirited child so much younger than himself who was his sister. And when their parents had died when they were still children he had guarded her all the more. And it was only to her could he talk freely, as if in confession. He spoke hesitantly, groping for phrases. At times there was a long gap as he silently continued to stare into the fire, the furrows on his brow etched deeper with the intensity of concentration. She watched his slightest gesture, not once interrupting him, her quiet patience matching his own.

He finished by relating the incident in the cottage with the sergeant, and after a lengthy pause asked, 'What should I do with him?'

She too let a long moment elapse while she studied the brooding face partly hidden in shadow. 'What can you do?'

'Nothing. He's free. Free to go. But he won't be released. He's intent on staying. I feel as if I'm now his prisoner. When it should be the other way around.' He paused. 'To stop him I'd have to shoot him.'

Though already knowing the answer, she nevertheless asked the question in order to keep him talking. 'And would you?'

He shook his head. 'I can't get his face out of my mind.

Streaked black and earth clinging to his beard. His hands too. As if he'd been trying to dig a hole in the ground to put himself. I saw a beast do that once after its young were dead. Clawing its way into the earth as if all it wanted to do was follow them.' He turned to look directly towards her. '"My son," he said. Back there on Slemish.'

'You couldn't possibly have known that.'

'No. But I knew almost at the time. When he insisted on a better place for a grave. I knew then there was something deep between us. Some feeling. And I knew he wasn't simply my prisoner.'

When he fell silent again she ladled some broth from the pot and handed it to him. He sat with the bowl clasped in both hands and only when she knocked the spoon against it did he slowly begin to eat.

'And after that I knew. During the trek. And I started saying to myself—I know. I know. But don't tell me. Don't tell me out loud.' He put the empty bowl aside and held out his glass to be refilled. 'You see, Cath, even though I knew, there was still doubt. There was still the possibility it wasn't his son. There was still doubt because it was still unsaid.'

She did not reply and allowed him to measure out the silence, trying to feel his pain as her own. Both had known too much to find any consolation in the platitudes of war.

'It does no good to know your enemy. Not like this.' He sipped his whisky, and then smiled. 'And you, Cath?'

She answered his smile. 'Much the same.'

'Young Cath?'

'In Dublin still. Safe, I think.'

'And the boys?'

'Still safe in America, thank God. There are times, Tidg . . . Times you begin to hate this country for what it does to you.'

She was now sitting staring into the fire, her hands in her lap. Watching her, he knew her loneliness as if it were his own, and his eyes strayed to the photographs on the wall. In the centre was the frank, smiling face of a young man, Sean, her husband, killed in the early days of the war against the British, who at least hadn't known the internecine fury which was to follow in its wake.

'What was his name?'

Instinctively he knew whom she meant. 'Ned, he calls him,' and immediately he wondered why he used the present tense, as though the son were still alive.

'Edward. A good sound to it.'

'Find another man, Cath. You're a young woman still and it's not good to be alone. Sean would have wanted it so.'

'Do you pick them off hedges?'

Inwardly he was grateful for this display of her biting wit, yet stubbornly pursued his own course. 'If I am to die I want the same for Maeve. It's not good for a woman to be alone.'

'The same? I'm tired, Tidg. The country's tired. We are tired.'

Now she was confessing. He probed gently, studying her face. 'There's hope.'

'No. There's no hope.'

'And the Republic's dead?'

'Not dead. It hasn't yet been born. The Republic's a dream, Tidg. A dream fading in blood and bitterness.'

'What news?'

'Only day to day. A successful attack here. A victory there. But as the days go on more defeats than victories. And more deaths among us.'

'But we're still fighting.'

'Yes. But everyone knows the outcome. The 'Staters will win. They're the real power because they're backed by England. We can't match that.'

'Yes. England. Getting Irishmen to do what they couldn't.'

'Does it matter who does it? It's been done.' She paused. 'You know some English soldiers deserted from the British army to join up with the Republicans? Now I hear that the 'Staters are rooting out the captured ones from the prison-camps to send back to English gaols.' She paused again. 'Part of the fee.'

Suddenly he thought of Childers, whom he hadn't thought of for some time. Childers, who was really English, yet the first

Irish Republican to be taken from his cell and shot. Deep in the soil, in his blood, in their blood, lay the issue of race. He'd known that. But not until now did he begin to understand the extent of its complexity. 'If the Free State has won, then we've lost all. In the north, still under Union and British rule, we'll be nothing. In the south too.'

'But who knows what shape the south'll take after the war ends? That's our only hope.'

'Even if it did change, I'm a northerner. Ulster is my home.'

'What are you going to do?'

He evaded her question. 'Tomorrow I'm going into town. With you.'

'To do what?'

'To listen.' Bending over her, he gently took her in his arms. 'Sleep, Cath. We both need sleep.'

But he didn't sleep much, nor had he expected to. In the back bedroom overlooking the yard he sat with his back against a wall in the same kind of posture he'd spent the two days in the cave, head thrown upwards, eyes slitted, face expressionless. Only once did he see signs of movement. At some time after midnight an army platoon crossed the railway lines and vanished among the huddle of buildings on the opposite side. Deliberately he picked out every detail he could, as though this professional exercise would help solve the uncertainty which now lay deep within him. Some hours later he quietly went to bed.

He heard her enter the room, his half-conscious mind weaving dream patterns round her movements. They were in a cave in the mountains, fighting the boy and the sergeant. They killed the boy, but were hemmed in by an army he couldn't see. Theirs was the flickering light, approaching to expose this hiding-place.

'Tidg.'

He was caught there, suspended, with true wakefulness eluding him, his will bending to delusion and fantasy. At last he woke with an exclamation, his hand reaching out to grasp his enemy. She sat on the edge of the bed, a lamp held low.

'You didn't sleep well?'

'Dreaming. I kept dreaming. Thinking.'

Still it was as though he were asleep. Or drugged. His own voice came from some distance away, like the voice of a stranger.

'Dreaming about what?'

'The boy. He was killed. And the sergeant . . .' The fragments drifted away from him.

She pushed him back. 'Go to sleep again. It's still dark. We've time in plenty. And you'll need your senses about you for today.'

When he finally wakened it was fully light. He lay for some minutes feeling the strength flow into his body and the sense of pleasurable ease in stretching his muscles which comes after proper rest. Parts of the dream lingered, and with consciousness of them came anxiety. The boy was a problem now as well. As the sergeant knew. Dressing, he went downstairs and joined her in the kitchen, where a breakfast of eggs and tea was simmering by the fire.

Watching him eat, she asked, 'Do you remember me waking you up?'

He thought for a moment, then shook his head. 'No.'

'You look tired too.'

He dipped the bread in the yoke of the egg. 'I shouldn't be. I've had plenty of rest in the mountains this past two days.'

'I don't mean that kind of tiredness.' She paused. 'You said you'd been dreaming. Dreaming and thinking.'

'Of the boy.'

She repeated what she'd asked the evening before. 'What are you going to do?'

'I don't know.'

She was silent for a while. 'It will only be a sacrifice, Tidg. If . . .'

He smiled gently. 'A sacrifice is sometimes necessary.'

'Some would say never necessary. Or to any purpose.'

Again he smiled. 'For those who aren't capable of sacrifice, even in thought, it is never necessary. And never serves any purpose.' He paused, carefully measuring his words. 'But any struggle is impossible without those who are capable of it. That I believe.'

Her voice was soft. 'Perhaps. And perhaps that's all right for those who know what they're doing. Not for those who don't.'

'The boy?'

Suddenly she stood up, ignoring his question, no longer wishing to resist his will. 'When do you want to go into town?'

'Now. And I'll be leaving again shortly after dark. It's over two hours to get back to the cave.'

They left the house in mid-morning and twenty minutes later were in the centre of town. She was certain that the police knew nothing of her own activity, never having bothered her again after bringing news of the death of her husband years before. It had happened south of Dublin, in the Wicklow hills. Even in her grief, she had seemed as surprised as they to discover that her husband had been one of Collins' men and active in the guerrilla campaign. All she knew was that he had gone to Dublin to find work. Her sons? They were already preparing to emigrate to America. Surely to God they'd find work there, for there was precious little of it in Ireland. And that meant there could be no other Republican activist in the family. They had accepted her words because, not only had they not returned, but in succeeding years she had never once been aware of watchful eyes or anything else that might have aroused her suspicions.

And so they walked together, though at first he tried to insist that they kept apart, meeting only once in town before returning. But she refused. She knew the town intimately, and would be able to talk much more plausibly if any incident did occur, backing up his story that he was just a hill farmer in town for the day to do one or two things, and a relation of hers.

And a hill farmer he was. Umkempt, unshaven, a bemused grin on his face, he slouched along at her side. A battered paddy hat sat on the back of his head, and a small sack dangled from his right hand, holding a collection of tools that badly needed sharpening and a few packets of seeds for an early plot because he wouldn't be in town again this side of spring. And the first time they were questioned and searched the soldier grinned at this dim-witted hillbilly for whom a visit to a collection of tin shacks would be a major social event.

He was glad he'd given in to her. Perhaps it was the months spent in the confines of the prison-ship that made him feel a sense of unease in the busy streets. People bustling around him, brushing past him, touching him, made him want to pull back into a doorway. And when two heavily armed soldiers stopped them he was aware of an edge of panic he'd never experienced before in such an encounter. But he carried his part well. Slouching, shuffling his feet, grinning, he pointed his finger in the direction of the sky and slurred some name neither of them could make out when asked where he came from. His companion chimed in, answering the questions for him, and the two soldiers shrugged and laughed at him and went their way.

Guiding him across the street she felt his arms tremble, and quickly glanced into his face.

'Whisky,' he whispered. 'I need whisky.'

In a narrow back street they slipped into a room of a spirit-grocer's, dimly lit, heavy with the smell of fresh sawdust. A small group of customers glanced at them briefly, then returned to their conversation. He ordered a full glass, and gratefully felt the whisky seep through him.

Her expression was quizzical. 'What's wrong?'

His back was to the counter, his face half-hidden, as he smiled down at her. 'Must have been too long in prison. I'm out of practice.'

'If you want to go back . . .'

'No. Just give me a few minutes.'

The whisky had been a good idea. In the street again he felt the unease deadened and his senses alert. No longer did the police and army uniforms press in upon him so forcibly that his reactions became confused. Now he deliberately slouched past them as close as possible, half-lingering, eyes and ears alert to the slightest gesture and word. Searched for a second time he breathed whisky fumes over the patrol, joking, asking was he at this new border that nobody knew where it was, or was there a border at all and how would you know it if you were at it, to hear one reply to the effect that he'd know he was there all right with the trouble he'd have, because he wouldn't be able to escape the army.

He followed her in and out of shops like some big obedient dog, but all the while picking scraps and phrases out of the air, analysing them, storing away what might be useful. Close to the market she stopped outside a large pub which took up most of a corner block.

'This one?'

'Where they mostly drink. And the one at the other end of the street.'

'You slip into a snug.'

He held the door open and she entered first. Just after midday, the bar was full. And full mostly of men in army uniform, the scattering of local people huddled in groups of their own. While walking to the bar he saw her slip into the smallest snug, close to the door, where he joined her a few minutes later carrying two whiskies and a jug of water. The only other occupant, an old woman with a deeply lined face, finding her peace suddenly disturbed, immediately gathered her bags and left.

He put the drink in front of her and smiled. 'As it's so rare we drink in town I thought I'd make this a toast.'

She raised her glass. '*Slainte*.'

'To us,' he said, smiling again and lightly touching her lips with his fingers.

The door of the snug was open and from where he was sitting he could see almost the full length of the bar. The insignia of the uniforms were as varied as the accents, the latter being mainly English and Scots. From the sack he took a sickle, his thumb running along the blade as if testing its battered edge. Head slightly bent, hat shading his forehead, he steadily watched the milling figures at the bar.

'Will I go on?'

'Yes. Give me about an hour and a half. I'll meet you outside at two. No later.' He felt a slight pressure on his arm and she brushed past him and left.

For well over half an hour he watched and listened. On a few occasions someone approached the snug but, on seeing the burly uncouth figure with his legs stretched across the doorway, moved away again. Patiently he sifted the talk floating through the air, eventually singling out a group of three soldiers at the centre of the bar, two in their early twenties and one some ten years older. Almost fully drunk, they were alternately laughing, singing and arguing about military matters. Replacing the blade in the sack, he waited his opportunity and, seeing a clear space beside them, approached the bar, ordered a pint of porter, and dropped the sack with a thump, hitting the heels of one of the younger men.

'Hey Paddy!'

He stretched out his arms, grinning, muttering unintelligibly, aware that the older man was eyeing him curiously.

'C'mon, for Cris' sake. He didn't mean nothing.' It was the second of the young men, pulling at the arm of his companion, who held up his fists as if to fight.

Still he stood with his arms out, grinning, trying to explain, until suddenly the fists were lowered and an arm fell across his shoulders.

'Paddy mate! Aren't we saving you from the Shiners?'

The soldier began to sing then, his companion joining in. He stood with his elbows on the bar, grinning, listening, nodding his head in enjoyment. The older man had turned away, no longer curious, and stood staring drunkenly into his glass.

'Aren't we, Paddy? Saving you from the Shiners? Fuck the Republic, says you! Whisky! Whisky!'

The barman set up three more glasses, and then a fourth. The young soldier pushed a glass towards him, then lifted it and pressed it against his mouth. 'For King and country!'

He took hold of the glass, spluttering at the pressure, watching the pair laugh loudly.

'We're in the war, Paddy! Saving you.'

'War?' he asked, his voice a slur.

'You don't hear much up in the hills, Paddy, do you? Don't you know there's a war on in Belleek?'

'Belleek? A right good town. Wasn't I there about twenty years ago?'

The soldier was leaning against him, arm still across his shoulders, laughing uproariously at this semblance of idiocy whose knowledge of the world was a small patch of ground and a few broken stones. The semblance of idiocy inanely laughed back and accepted more whisky. With several carefully chosen phrases he discovered their regiment and their tours of duty on the border, and, more importantly, the main posts on the border and those areas subject only to patrols. Becoming sentimental, both began talking about their personal lives and their desire to return to England. He stood, visualising that terrain which was now border country, the lush lough lands of Erne where in summer the tall reeds ran across the surface of the shimmering water before the Atlantic breezes and fell into Donegal Bay, and where the pools and inlets were quivering rich in trout and salmon. Derry was now cut off from its hinterland of Donegal, Strabane too. Never had the country been so divided. Here in the west of this new northern State poverty would be as before, or worse. With its large nationalist areas it would remain a threat to Unionist control. Again he felt that racial hatred stir within him, a gnawing hatred which defied the mind to analyse. Immured in past centuries it seemed somehow to be impersonal, something beyond himself which used his own person as a vehicle for its expression. Beneath drooped eyelids he watched the clear young faces. He had no hatred for them, but for what their battle dress symbolised, signified. He warmed to their talk, to their fresh young blood and hopes, yet knew he would kill both without a moment's regret. It's not good to know your enemy.

They had forgotten him. The arm was no longer across his shoulder. Engrossed in each other's talk they didn't notice as he gradually eased away. Finishing his drink with a last surreptitious look around the bar, he lifted his sack and left. In the street again he was the same slouching comic figure as he walked by her side, shoulders bent, hat falling off his head, the sack slung across one shoulder.

127

As she raked out the fire he took some hot water and washed and shaved. It might be the last time he would be able to do so in comfort for a long time to come. Darkness was already falling though it wasn't yet three o'clock. A few hours' rest and he would leave in the early evening. He watched her arrange the heavy blanket across the window before she lit the lamp, then sat down as she poured out two bowls of broth. They hadn't yet spoken since meeting outside the pub, as though each was acknowledging in silence the impending leave-taking which might be the last.

He reached out to touch her face. 'Well?'

'News was coming in of a break-out in Athlone. A large number, it's said.'

'So we're still fighting?'

'Yes.' She paused. 'But still losing. It's got worse.' She paused again. 'And you know what the break-out will mean?'

'More executions.'

She nodded. 'And anywhere in the country. It doesn't matter to the 'Staters now who they execute. They've even started to execute their own men who came over to us. The country's rank with bitterness, Tidg. Bitterness and hate and exhaustion.'

He was silent for a while. 'Where's the main fighting?'

'In the south, mostly. Cork. Kerry. Athlone. Dundalk. Limerick.'

'And Donegal?'

'Seems quiet except for beyond Derry.' She paused. 'What will you do?'

'I'll decide when I cross the border. It might be better to go south.'

Her voice was soft. 'There's talk of a cease-fire. That Dev and the council will order a cease-fire.' Her voice was louder. 'They'll have to, Tidg, if they want to have any of us left.'

He smiled, and again touched her face with his fingertips. 'No one's ever managed to finish us off yet.'

'You're going, then?'

'Yes,' he said, even though he was still unsure. He wouldn't leave her with uncertainty. That wasn't right.

Their leave-taking, a little while later, was perfunctory. A brief embrace, a whispered goodbye, and he was standing outside the yard door listening to the sound of the boulder being rolled into place. Quickly he crossed the embankment and followed the railway lines, returning the way he had come. Only once, on the other side of town, did he have to stop. The voices passed some distance away. Then he was climbing into the hills, driving himself on at a fast pace. His body felt light and hard and fit, in contrast to his mind, which was still fogged with doubt and confusion. He welcomed the wind which swept down from the mountains to fan his face, as well as the light rain it brought which trickled from forehead to chin, as if the elements would conspire to bring sharpness to his brain.

He reached the cache and sat beside it, momentarily visualising the sergeant and the boy. The cave was less than half a mile away. He remembered what he'd said to the sergeant. If I don't return, you're in charge. My enemy. Idly he wondered what was in the sergeant's mind, what the latter would do if he didn't return. Would he take the boy into the barracks in Omagh and then begin a hunt in the mountains? An image of himself came to mind, of being tracked across the country. But now it seemed unreal, like watching someone else. Or would the sergeant simply walk away, walk back the way he had come, leaving the boy to make his own choice? There was doubt in the other's mind also. Of that he felt sure. Confused, it would be so easy now just to stand up and walk away. To go back to the farm. They would come for him eventually, and in prison there would at least be life. The Republic's a dream, Tidg, she'd said. A dream fading in blood and bitterness. He saw the dorsal fin of the dolphin, himself swimming across the narrow lough, the lights of the prison-ship suddenly ablaze again on the dark water. Was it life? And what would the sergeant think if he didn't return? 'Back there on Slemish. My son you killed. For what?'

It was his senses that made the decision, or so it seemed. The cache was open and his hands were groping inside before he was fully aware of his own actions. But now, with each careful, deliberate movement, he felt the rift in his mind healing, his purpose returning. Slowly he took the pistol and the sergeant's revolver, loading each in turn, tucking one into his belt and slipping the other into his pocket. Then he lifted the .303 and inserted a full magazine. Pausing, his fingers sought what had first caught his eye when he'd opened the cache the morning before, and he grasped the stock of the Parabellum. He rubbed the oil from the machine-pistol and began loading the drum, the weapon bringing the final sense of what he always had been and always would be, a Republican fighter. Thoughts of youth came, making him smile: of the old poteen-besotted priest, broken in body yet still clear in mind, who had seen in him a strong mind and will and who had educated him first at the hedge school and later in the church hall, leaving him with a passion for books and thought like the quiet passion he had for his mountain home. *Si vis pacem para bellum.* If you want peace, prepare for war.

Hurrying now, he separated the different kinds of ammunition, filling a cloth bag which he hung from one shoulder. From his other shoulder the Parabellum hung by its strap. This was more to his purpose than the light hunting rifle which they'd carried previously, and which he now left behind. He found himself humming softly. The song seemed to fill his whole being. His hands and body were now quick, alert, scornful of error. Before sealing the cache he placed in the centre of the remaining guns a note he'd written earlier in the day, with the information that he was crossing the Fermanagh/Donegal border to join up with Republican forces. It gave his Brigade and rank, a salute to the Republican dead, and was signed simply—*Tidg—29 December, 1922.*

The sergeant was the first to see the man return. He was sitting on a boulder, the greatcoat wrapped round him, as the man emerged out of the darkness with barely a sound. Though his face was expressionless, the sergeant quickly noted that the .22 rifle had been replaced by a German machine-pistol, and he knew. The man paused for a moment, looking at him, and then from behind came the boy's voice in greeting.

'You're back. And what's the news?'

'We're leaving.'

The sergeant stood up. 'Where to?'

'We'll go along the top of Lough Erne. And cross the border north of Belleek.'

'And then?' the boy asked.

'Most of the fighting seems to be in the south. So we'll probably go south into Sligo.'

'What was it like in Omagh?' the boy asked.

The man ignored him. 'Let's clear up the cave. We're leaving now.'

In about an hour the cave was swept and the boulder rolled back into place. Carefully the man brushed the rocky path in the fissure, kneeling in the darkness, before joining the other two where they waited some dozen yards away. Beside them lay the sack holding what was left of their provisions. Turning to the boy, he asked, 'How do you feel?'

'As good as ever.'

The man looked into the boy's glowing face and bright eyes. With the long rest he was completely recovered. He was silent for a long moment, then suddenly said, 'You're both free to go. Now.'

The boy was startled. 'Go where?'

'Wherever you want.'

'And the Republic?'

'Is still fighting. But will be defeated.'

'Are you sure?'

'Certain.'

'And you?'

'I'm going where I said I'd go.'

Bending, the boy picked up the sack and tossed it over his shoulder. 'I'll not stay behind now.'

The man turned to the sergeant. 'And you?'

The sergeant slowly shook his head, saying nothing.

'If you attempt to betray us now, I'll have to shoot you. And once over the border you're on your own. That's as far as you go with us.'

The sergeant stood looking, still saying nothing, as the others moved away, the man leading. At a question from the boy the man stopped and turned, a smile on his face, and tossed the .303 to his companion. The boy caught the rifle in mid-air and tucked it under his arm, his eyes briefly meeting the sergeant's. And as the latter saw the quick, eager face and watched him turn his back and walk away he felt a numbing sense of grief, as though he had lost another. Then he began to follow.

Duncan

Dawn is breaking and still they keep ahead of me, rarely looking back. During the eight hour march I judge we've travelled roughly twenty-five miles. The man keeps up a steady pace and I can almost hear him calculating our steps with precision as hour follows hour. Early I see a faint glow to the south which I take to be Omagh and the sound and smell of the barracks comes easily to mind. Always we keep to the high ground, cutting through the most difficult passes, hiding in gorges when we can. Even if our presence has been discovered he doesn't expect to be followed here. He is a good soldier, I think, and with the Parabellum swinging at his waist I begin to think more and more of the Somme.

In the morning sky a solitary speck swoops and circles, coming closer, and I can see them both watching it also. It's a falcon and as I join them on the peak it drops below us in a long dive leaving us with our first sight of the ocean. And there it is. Beneath us lies Lough Erne, closed in from the vastness of the Atlantic by a small strip of land. I watch the falcon until it's out of sight and think of it making for the sea-cliffs of Donegal just as I've often watched them swoop over the Antrim cliffs to the east and I look at the two figures and think of the prison-ship.

'The Blue Stack mountains.'

The man is pointing to the north, where still higher peaks can be seen floating in and out of mist. In his expression is a sense of possession, a oneness with the land and a possession that tolerates no breach and then I remind myself that he's a man from the mountains and this is his home. More than that, the home of his people before it was my people.

The boy rests the butt of his rifle on the ground. 'Donegal!'

The man is pointing again and there's that rare smile on his face as he puts his arm across the boy's shoulders. 'And Donegal Bay. We'll soon be there.'

'What now?' I ask.

'Still no travelling during daylight. We go to ground.' For a moment he pauses, looking round, then says, 'Wait here.'

He's gone longer than I expect. The boy is talking eagerly, pointing, asking me about this and that. But I'm in no mind for talk. His excitement jars on my own mood, a mood bound up with our parting as though I now no longer wish the end of this unwilling trek. When the man returns his face is a mask as before. Curtly he commands the boy to stay where he is and beckons to me and tells me to come.

It is a cave as before, though one which has been hewn out and enlarged, and not very long ago. The marks of spades and picks still glint on the dullish rock. The body is lying face upwards in the centre, one hand still clutching the groin and the other a rifle, the legs partly bent. That wasn't its original resting-place and I trace out where the man has dragged it from a corner. Part of the flesh is eaten away and I find myself thinking of rats and of one demented soul who would amuse himself by tying morsels of food across the muzzle of his rifle and when a rat started to eat would pull the trigger. That was before he threw his rifle away and deliberately walked towards a German machine-gun.

'Who?'

'One of us.'

'A Republican?'

'Yes.'

He nods.

'You knew him?'

'Yes.'

It's hard to tell his age because there's so little left of his features. I look out of the cave and down the hillside in an idle unfeeling fashion watching him crawl hopefully upwards with his lifeblood trickling into the sparse mountain soil to lie here with his eyes gradually dimming, thinking when he could and waiting to die. For how long?

'You'll have to break his hands and fingers to get the rifle free,' I hear myself saying. 'And his legs if you want to lay him out straight.'

'No. We bury his rifle with him.'

'We?' A thought provokes me. 'Why are you protecting the boy?'

'Protecting?'

'Shouldn't he be here to see this? It's his war too now. And maybe this'll be his death.'

A spasm crosses his face and I rejoice. He moves to the entrance of the cave and turns, his voice sharp. 'Drag him outside.'

In the full light of day the body looks even more hideous and I wait until the man comes down from the peak with the boy at his heels. The latter stops beside the corpse and then quickly spins round and vomits, his companion holding him by the shoulder.

I catch the boy's eye. 'One of your comrades.'

'Leave it!'

The man raises his gun and for a moment I expect a blow but he abruptly walks off towards the cave and comes back a few minutes later with a spade which he throws at my feet.

'Dig!'

I toss the spade to the boy. The shaft hits him on the side and it falls. 'You dig,' I say, and pause, watching him. 'It might be your own grave you're digging.'

We wrap the body in a blanket. I help the boy, using my hands and a piece of slated rock as an implement. It's hard work, hewing a grave out of the tough mountain earth, and I think of the man on his farm with the same hard ground to work. Soon we are sweating though the boy's face is pinched and set.

'What're you thinking?' I ask.

'Nothing.'

Still I goad him. 'That this might be you?'

This time he ignores me and we finish the job and level the ground as best we can, with the boy putting a few stones in the shape of a cross in the centre of the grave. The man is sitting with his back against a rock and the machine-pistol lying in his lap, studying the country through his field-glasses. Idly I begin to wonder where he got this new weapon and think of the trenches again, maybe because of the gun's make. When the news of the rebellion in Dublin came up the line we knew then that not even the outcome of a great war would change this one.

'You're still free to go.' He doesn't look up when he says it as though he now truly wishes that I did go.

'You forget. I want to see you like the one we've just buried.'

'That you won't see.'

At first I take his remark to mean that he has total confidence in himself, and then I wonder if it might be that he has made a decision. 'Does that mean both of us?'

'Yes.'

I turn to the boy. 'Well?'

He hesitates and again I rejoice. A feeling of triumph is mine, the struggle between my captor and myself isn't yet finished. I glance towards where he is still sitting and expect to find him watching us and am disappointed. All I see is his back as he still scours the land below through the glasses.

Awkwardly the boy stands with the toe of his right boot stirring the soil, passing the rifle from hand to hand. 'What regiment were you in?

'Regiment?'

'In the trenches. In France.'

'The Ulster Division. The 36th.'

'You mean the UVF,' the boy says.

'The Ulster Volunteer Force,' I answer. 'Yes. Most of us. Not all.'

'Not all?' The boy pauses, staring at the ground. 'You were never all. Aren't all now. All of us wanted Ireland free. And we voted more than you. But you killed us to stop us.'

'Answer him.'

It's the man speaking. He lolls sideways, the field-glasses dangling at his chest, a strange smile quirking his mouth. I turn away.

'Tell me about them. The trenches.'

'I've never been able to tell,' I say.

Still the boy persists. 'And after that?'

'I was in the south. I told you that.'

'Yes. With the British army. With the Black-and-Tans. Killing Republicans.'

It is true. That is what I did. But I make no answer.

'Like him up there. Like him we've just buried. Maybe even like your own son. Like Ned.'

A youthful face passes before my eyes and a grave on a barren hillside. The hill at my back. But rather than provoking me as I thought they must do, the boy's words dull my brain. Suddenly I'm cold with a damp coldness that strikes to the bone and I sit down and put the greatcoat tightly round me and hear the boy being told to go to the cave and prepare some food. The sun is shining on Lough Erne below, sending blinding flashes of light dagger-like from the water and on the endless stretch of the ocean. Scenes begin to invade my mind that until now I had blocked from memory.

'Here.'

A whisky bottle is thrust into my hand as the man changes position and sits nearby and only then do I become aware that I'm visibly trembling.

'Don't tell me you're getting the fever too?'

Despite myself I laugh but it's a laugh with tears in it. 'No,' I find myself saying, 'hardly that.'

'I didn't think so. Having come through the Somme I don't expect you to get the fever here.'

A salute from my enemy. As I to him. My God, my God. 'And the fever didn't kill the boy,' I say. 'Though it seems you are going to.'

'The boy isn't yours. You've lost him.'

'I know that now,' I say.

His voice is soft. 'Nor is he mine.'

I wait. But as he remains silent, I ask, 'What happens when we cross the border?'

'You'll be all right. The Free Staters won't shoot at you. You're not part of their war now.' He pauses. 'It would do the new government in the south no good if their troops started killing police in the north.'

Again he admits it openly. And this time with a tone of finality. The Republic is defeated. He feels it, knows it. 'And you?' I ask.

'Me?'

As he says nothing further I ask, 'Why, Tidg?' and then realise that it's the first time I've called him by name.

He smiles. 'Why the sacrifice in the trenches?'

'But we won.'

His voice is still soft, almost like a woman's. 'It seems to me that no one won.' He pauses again. 'Like us now.'

'Him we buried,' I say. 'Did you know him?'

He nods. 'His name was Brennan. Three weeks ago he left to cross the border. I learned that in Omagh.' He lifts the field-glasses to study the landscape. 'Your people were on to him. The police.'

And must have been responsible for shooting him, I think. With his wounds it is doubtful if he'd managed to come this far from the border. But, as though reading my thoughts, he turns to me.

'Hard to know which side shot him. I've known him to travel twenty miles with a bullet in his back. He was tough like that.'

'Yes,' I say. 'Troops of the Free State will be concentrated on the border too.'

He nods. 'And they have to be, if you think about it. Isn't the line of the border still disputed? Even by the Free Staters? If the British Army has to be there to see the 'Staters don't push the border back, then the 'Staters equally have to make sure the Unionists don't grab even more land than they already have. Which they're already trying to do.' He pauses for a moment. 'Which makes things on the border even more tricky for me.'

138

'Only you?' I ask, but my question is ignored. Then I say, 'You're not the only ones who didn't want Ireland divided.'

'But now it is.' He smiles. 'And how are you going to keep it like that? There'll always be places that'll not rest peaceful for long. Derry. Fermanagh. Tyrone. Other places too. They'll always want to break away. I know it. You know it. And in order to keep them within the border this territory will have to be turned into an armed camp. Like it is now. And that means what I've already said. No one has won. A country can't be an armed camp forever.'

'But we'll survive.'

'In what way? And for this now, what if the day comes when the British no longer back you?'

I stare at the lough below and say nothing.

'We're not stupid men, you and I. We're not those who beat drums and shout without thinking. In this new State my kind will be nothing. Just as we also were nothing. Just as we always must be nothing. Because if we had power we might choose to go our own way. Which isn't your way. You live in Ireland and refuse to commit yourself to it. We live in Ireland and refuse to commit ourselves to anything else. To us Britain is as foreign a country as Germany.'

'What are you talking about?'

It's the boy, coming down the hill behind us unnoticed.

The man's voice is gruff. 'About war. And about something to eat.' He stands up. 'And about how you haven't much time to learn how to use a rifle properly.'

We sit outside the cave, chewing the dry shrivelled scraps which are all that remain of the food we brought from the cottage. No hunting, he'd said. The guns are too heavy and there's no time now for snares. He's right. Early in the afternoon he points and hands me the glasses. On a road far below a long convoy of British army lorries winds its way towards the border. It's like being in France again, though watching the wrong side, and for a moment I see the scene through his eyes. This is the enemy. The uniform I once wore. The uniform I wear now. It's as if I am his companion and I think of the dead Republican soldier buried nearby whose only symbol of allegiance is the rifle still clutched in his hand. Of Ned, whose only symbol was a cap and a greatcoat. But now I feel no hard edge of anger and think of myself in that moment of madness when I dug into the earth for my son.

'Will they never end?'

It's the boy speaking as he peers through the glasses which I handed to him. Even with the naked eye I can see the dull shapes moving below and in my mind watch them swerving to a stop and the mule trains begin, because the mules are better at getting the supplies to the front through the gore and the mud and the shellholes.

'When do we move?' the boy asks.

'Tonight. We cross the top of Lough Erne at Boa Island.' The man takes the glasses from him and studies the convoy. 'But if there's this much activity about we might be delayed further. North of Belleek we should manage to avoid the patrols. Then we'll go south past Ballyshannon. But you'd better get some rest. And the cave might be warmer than out here.'

I follow the boy and sit close to him at the entrance of the cave. Sheltered from the wind, the sun seems warmer. The darkness of the inside of the cave isn't inviting and then I think that the boy's reluctance to go inside might be because of its last occupant.

'What will you do when we cross the border?'

It's the first time the boy has asked me of my intentions. Even in my own mind I hadn't bothered about that question as if the goal was still remote. 'Find the nearest authority and get myself back to where I came from. The Free Staters won't kill me,' I say, echoing the other. 'That would do them no good.'

'But they'll kill us,' the boy says. 'As you will.'

'You've lost,' I say. 'Your cause is lost. Didn't you hear him say so? Even he doesn't want you to go on. If he had he wouldn't have given you the choice to go back.'

'And what choice do you give me?'

'One better than throwing your life away.'

'One better than throwing my life away?' The boy is silent for a long time and then says, 'I've listened to you both. I've heard you both. I believe him when he says we'll be nothing. We'll always get the least. And if anything ever happens the police will come banging on our doors with guns. What do I go back to?'

'You're a seaman,' I say. 'You'll be well away from anything that happens.'

'Because I'll be afraid to be around if they do?'

I look at him but his face is turned away from me, my words still sounding in my ears in their harsh stupidity. A country that can't be a home. In him I sense a depth more than his years and as I keep watching the solemn boyish face I think it might be that which makes him go on, knowing the futility of the choice offered him. In the trenches I met his kind also. I remember them now. Boys who walked out carelessly to die as if to show the futility of the lives they'd been given. And from under a steel helmet I see a pair of blue eyes squinting at me still: I don't believe in you any more. I don't believe in anything you tell me. I'm not fighting for anything. I'm not even fighting. I don't even believe it matters how I die because you've given me no true reason why I die. All you've given me is a trap. If I go on, the enemy will kill me. If I refuse to go on, my own side will kill me.

It was like a bayonet in my flesh, that steady look which had neither anger nor fear nor any feeling whatsoever.

'Do you still hate him?'

'Hate him?'

'For killing your son.'

I shake my head. 'Maybe I didn't hate him even then.'

'In the cottage. Why didn't you kill him?'

Again I shake my head. 'Maybe I was tired of seeing so much killing.'

'You don't know much, old man.'

'True,' I say. 'I don't know much.'

He looks at me and smiles at this, then goes into the cave to fetch some blankets. Tossing one to me he rolls himself up in the other and stretches out. I can't see the man from this position and think he must still be near the peak, watching the land

141

below. Again I wonder idly where he got the machine-pistol from and see myself in 1914 in Larne, waiting for the guns to be brought in, and hear the talk of the steamer now on the high seas running the British blockade. The swift unloading as the police surrounded the decoy ship in Belfast and the guns being driven to Tyrone and Fermanagh in the west, where they'd be needed most. We seemed invulnerable then to keep this country under the king and here I am in Tyrone and Fermanagh with my invulnerability threadbare and a sleeping boy listening to my confession.

For I brought a different face back from the Somme, the face of futility speaking the words of the son against the father. In the days of the guerrilla war it followed me too, haunted me. Wherever I looked, I saw it. I saw it in the flames of the big houses burning, flickering on the backs of the owners as they slipped out of a country they'd never belonged to, leaving it to burn, burn. I saw it among the flames of burning cottages and villages pillaged in retaliation. On the faces of owners who could not flee. Traced in the flowing red pools of the assassinated in the streets. That is why I do not hate him. That is why I did not kill his son. His face was the face of accusation. The other one's too. And in Ned's face. You have betrayed me.

Why are you crying, old man?
    Why am I not?
    Can't you sleep?
    No.
    What are you thinking?
    About before the war started. The Great War. About the gun-running in Larne.
    I remember it.
    How old were you?
    About ten.
    I wish my other son had been that age.
    Your other son? You had two?
    Yes. Two.

What happened to him?

He's dead too.

How?

In the trenches. With me.

What was he fighting for?

He didn't know. That's what he told me before he died. He was dying for nothing. And it didn't matter who killed him. Both sides were his enemies.

Was he shot?

Bayoneted.

Did you find him?

Yes. Dead.

He was wise.

Like you? To die?

You old men kill us. Your own sons.

What were you thinking?

About the dolphin again.

Tell me about it. Like you told me about it in the other cave.

It's just that a dolphin is a beautiful thing. And one helped me to escape. To be so beautiful and so free and not to have to think. That must be life. What it's like to be alive.

And the beast has more life than us?

Why not? They don't have to kill each other. Hate each other.

If only it were so easy.

Old men always say that. But can't tell us why it's so difficult.

Do you know why you're fighting?

No. Like your sons.

Then I am the one who is condemned. Him up there too.

I become aware of the boy watching me curiously and suddenly ask, 'Were you sleeping?'

'No. I couldn't.'

'It's often like that,' I say. 'Before a battle. Before shooting. You'll soon be in the fighting.' I pause for a moment to see if he'll reply, then say, 'I was thinking about your dolphin.'

'And I was thinking about a woman.'

'Have you had a woman?'

'You asked me that before.' Embarrassed, the boy hesitates. 'I was thinking about a girl. It was in a port in China. With all the lights of the sampans and the docks and the eating places. I was taken to where she was. It was behind a house. But she was in a cage. It was like a cage. And she could only eat when she got some money. And she could only get money by . . .'

'Selling her body,' I say gently.

'Yes.'

'And then?'

'I just sat there watching her eat. And then I wanted to run away. But she wouldn't let me. And she kept singing to me. Even afterwards. And telling me about some other sailor that loved her. And who'd come back to see her again. Just as I would come back. Even when I was sleeping I could still feel her lips close to me. Still hear her singing. She was beautiful like a dolphin. But a dolphin somebody had caught and put in a pond.'

'Yes,' I say. 'There's many different kinds of captivity.'

> *O love is kind, to the least of men,*
>   *Heave awa', 'eave awa',*
> *Though he be but a drunken tar,*
>   *Heave awa', awa'.*
>
> *Far from land, and the sight of man,*
>   *Heave awa', 'eave awa',*
> *Come all who love a sailorman,*
>   *Heave awa', awa'.*
>
> *Take me to that starlight main,*
>   *Heave awa', 'eave awa',*
> *O I was happy with her then,*
>   *Heave awa', awa'.*
>
> *In the comfort of her bed,*
>   *Heave awa', 'eave awa',*
> *Let me lie until I'm dead,*
>   *Heave awa', awa'.*

The clear soft voice of the boy lingers in the air. Dusk is falling and far out across the ocean the stars begin to shine. A sound makes me turn and I see the man crouching nearby, the expression on his face showing that he too has heard the boy singing and has been drawn irresistibly by the boy's natural delicacy. Unknown to him he has caught the haunting simplicity of the song and its sense of being shut away from life. I want to say something but can find nothing to say and it's the boy who finally speaks.

'I learned that song from a girl.'

"What girl?' the man asks, as though he too feels that he must say something but can find nothing else.

'A girl in a cage. Like the cage we were in. The cage on board the ship.' He stops for a moment, then says, 'You know, it's funny. All the time we've been walking, running, I keep thinking we're still in a cage. Only the bars of the cage are barrels of guns. Maybe that's why I just keep going. That one day I might escape and be free. Like a dolphin. Like the dolphin that showed us the way through the wires.'

Again we are silent until the man stands up. 'Rest some more,' he says. 'We'll be late moving. There's too many troops still on the road below.'

As the man moves away again I try to get the boy to talk some more, but he lies back and starts singing softly as though he has closed us both out and I'm left with thoughts that won't go away. To be like a beast with no mind or memory to dig and inflame the scabs of our wounds. I can tell him nothing. Nor can the other. He knows us both now and knows we have nothing to say. Like the boy in the trenches with a bayonet in his chest. You have nothing more to tell me. And the other one on Slemish and trying to bury my face in the earth like a beast already without knowing it. Trying to blot out the memory to still the pain. Like the last fall of light showing in the red streaks among the western clouds welcoming in the night, the red streaks of receding memory welcomed by a mind seeking its own night and darkness. In the comfort of her bed, the boy sings, let me lie until I'm dead. Alone on a creaking ship on a never ending ocean, a sea-shanty for the likes of us. You too, old man. What more do you want than that? She'll be at the window with the lichen round it, staring out into the darkness with a week gone already not yet knowing that Ned is no more. The man's too. The big woman in the cottage sitting by the fire waiting to hear that he is no more. The girl in the cage singing. A prostitute before she was the age of ten. Take me to that starlight main. But yes. There's more kinds of captivity than one. These great events are history. And in these great events I sit in a wilderness listening to a song. We might as well have the boy on a stone with a knife at his heart and ourselves as the high priests. Listen, son, the Pope's a Protestant and the Kaiser's the Holy Ghost and the Czar's a refugee and Lloyd George is the King of Heaven and it's the fire next time when we'll all be free. Why was my son killed? Because some other man needed his boots. I have nothing more to tell you.

'You're crying, old man,' the boy says.

I shake my head. 'No, son. I'm looking for my sanity. I lost it on that other hillside when I laughed. You were insane then. With the fever.'

'I don't understand.'

'No more do I.'

'Why do you stay, old man?' Again he looks at me curiously. 'You know you can go.'

'Maybe I've chosen to be a sacrifice. Like you.'

'Is that what I am?'

'Yes,' I say.

'Then maybe that's all I can be.'

'We're leaving.' The man stands above us and points towards the cave. 'Close it up.'

'I'm hungry,' the boy says, getting to his feet.

We both watch as the man crosses to a solitary tree and hacks at it with the knife. Coming back, he hands a piece of bark to the boy.

'Eat it. It'll fill your belly. That's what the monks did when they were hiding from the invaders. What the people of the famine did when they didn't have a corpse to eat.'

He looks at me when he says it but I make no response. The boy throws the bark on the ground and turns away. I follow him and we roll up our blankets and seal the cave. He pauses for a moment in the shadow of a rock and lights the butt of a cigarette, then passes it to me. More as a gesture of closeness I accept and take a deep pull which makes me feel slightly sick yet grateful for the bitter tang in my mouth and throat. The man is beside us again, picking up the .303 to rub the metal parts with damp soil.

'Why that?' the boy asks, watching him.

'Keep the shiny parts dull. We don't want a trick of light telling somebody where we are.' He throws the rifle to the boy and starts to make his way down the hillside.

We begin to leave the mountains behind but the going is slow. Not because of the terrain this time but because the man stops every few miles to crouch for a long time and listen. Twice we hear the rumble of lorries in the distance and both times he leaves us to reconnoitre, returning up to an hour later. And on both occasions I study the boy, feeling that it's no longer a matter of changing his mind but that I must save him despite himself. Perhaps this decision has been made by his own mood transmitting itself to me. In the past few hours we've all changed. The trek is over. Their goal is in sight. In the boy there's a tense nervous excitement. And in the man's actions there's no longer any hesitation or sense of divided will as though all possible questions had been faced and answered; unlike myself. Now he is as I had first seen him and as the boy had first seen him on the prison-ship, a mask hiding an intense concentration and determination. The cracks I had noticed a few days earlier are no longer there and it's then I realise how deeply I had wanted to see him break.

Some hours before daylight we reach Lough Erne. I know the land well now and recall that it's only six months ago in summer when I was last here among the fifty thousand and more troops and police crowded into this little strip of border territory with the soldiers yelling for the Republican hill tribes in Donegal to attack. The scenes jostle together in my mind as I notice the man waving us to huddle down among the long grass and stones of the lough shore before vanishing into the darkness and I crouch listening to the wind ruffle the surface of the water and see the black shape of Boa Island a little way off. Soon he appears again, walking in the shallows, a boat riding the water at his side.

The nervousness in the boy's voice is more obvious than before as he asks, 'Where are we?'

'The border,' I say. 'It's about two miles north and ten west.'

'Then we'll cross it the night.'

'No,' the man says. 'Not the night. It's too close to daylight and we want to know what's facing us.'

We climb into the boat and sit low as the man paddles out, using a single oar at the stern. Hugging the shallows, we move along the northern shore of the island, making for the western end. The boat is pulled up before day begins to break and is concealed.

'Tomorrow we'll be over the border, old man,' the boy whispers, 'and then we'll be free.'

'You forget easy,' I say. 'You'll hardly be free with a civil war going on.'

He doesn't reply to that and I sit watching the sky getting lighter. The wind across the lough is cold and I soon feel numb and tired. I didn't sleep the day before, I remember, and the thought makes my tiredness increase. The man leaves us and comes back to say there's no trace of anyone else around and we'll stay the day on the island. Finding a place where the rocks act as a windbreak, I make up a bed of rushes and grass and am soon asleep.

I wake up again feeling even more numb and stiff and with a rumbling in my head. As I try to get up a hand pushes me back again. It's the boy, his face close to mine and showing fear. At this point the island is only a few hundred yards from the main shore and on the other side I can see lorries and armoured cars passing. Every so often one stops with a cheerful shouting and singing.

'It's been going on for hours,' the boy says. 'They must be changing the garrison or something.'

The man is lying outstretched, hidden by the rushes, watching the convoy through the field-glasses. I note it's almost dark again, which means I must have slept a good six hours. The tiredness is replaced by hunger and then I remember there's nothing left to eat. Night comes and at intervals the lorries still rumble by, their lights beaming through the odd clusters of trees to light up the water. Twice the man makes preparations to leave and stops again at the sound of distant engines.

'It'll not be tonight we're leaving,' he says finally. 'There's too much going on over there.'

'And how long do we stay?' the boy asks.

'As long as need be. Sleep. That way your belly can't tell you it's hungry.'

The man moves away again, going towards the water, and I sit watching the stars showing through broken cloud, the boy and Ned and a dolphin merging into one another with the sound of the boy singing. In the cottage the girl is singing and I stand with the gun to his son's head watching him lying unconscious on the floor and wonder why I feel no bitterness. A heavy thud on my leg shatters the images and the dream vanishes as I roll over and get up. A khaki canvas bag is lying beside me and the man is crouching a few yards away.

'What's this?' I ask.

'A present. A present from the enemy.' He swings the Parabellum by the strap and places it on the ground. 'But it depends whose enemy.'

I open it. It's a soldier's field-bag, complete with tinned beef, biscuits and first-aid dressings.

'Did you never have to eat German rations in the trenches?'

'Yes,' I say, and empty the contents of the bag on the ground as the boy joins us and kneels beside me.

The man cuts open the tins with the knife, ignoring the boy's questions. We eat in silence and then he throws a packet of cigarettes on top of the bag. 'These too,' he says, 'a present.'

As we light up the boy asks again, 'What did you find out?'

149

'Enough to know what to do. We leave tomorrow night. About midnight. Going slow and keeping an eye out for patrols it'll take us about two hours. We cross a mile or so north of Belleek. Well away from where most of the troops will be.' He pauses, then says, 'It's New Year's Day tomorrow. There'll be a lot of drinking going on. It'll be a good time to cross.'

'What about him?' the boy asks.

'We leave him behind. Tomorrow night.' He's silent for a while, then says, 'You'd better get as much rest as you can. It might be a long trek south before we meet up with our own kind.'

'There'll be no relaxing of patrols if that's what you're hoping for,' I say.

As he makes no reply I'm about to get up when the pressure of his hand on my arm makes me wait and I sit listening to the boy splashing at the water's edge. The man checks the drum of the machine-pistol and then unloads the revolver and tosses it on the ground beside me. Then he checks the pistol also and pushes it back into his belt. The splashing ceases and the boy moves up the bank to bed down. The engine of an armoured car sounds somewhere on the main shore and it isn't until it ceases that he speaks.

'You'll find ammunition for your gun in the boat on the other side. I'll be taking the boy's rifle.'

'I don't understand,' I say.

'The boy too. This is as far as he goes.'

'And how are you going to stop him now?'

'You are going to stop him.' From a pocket he takes out my silver watch. 'This is yours too. But the knife I'll keep.'

'What's in your mind?' I ask.

'The boy isn't yours. Nor is he mine. That we agreed.'

'Yes,' I say.

'With what's happening on the other side he'll either be shot or caught. And maybe even shot when caught.'

I nod in agreement and sit turning the watch over and over in my hand, thinking that now I've no one to pass it on to yet feeling a sense of relief which blurs my sight.

'You'll promise me one thing.'

'Which is?' I ask.

'He won't be your captive either. Get him away from here. Get him on a ship. You've the power to do that, haven't you?'

'Yes,' I answer. 'I've the power to do that.'

'Good,' he says. 'Tomorrow I'll leave alone. Long before midnight. By the time he knows I've gone it'll be too late to follow me. Anyway you'll have your gun and he won't know it's unloaded. The boat'll be on the other side. It's so narrow here it won't be difficult to get across without it.'

'Still don't trust me?' I ask.

'Not when you've been cheated of seeing me die by my own kind.' Then he says, 'Thanks.'

'For what?' I ask.

'In the cottage. My son.'

I don't answer him and we are silent for a long time after that. I know what's in his thoughts and am ready when he tries to speak.

'I'm only sorry that—'

'No,' I say quickly. 'No. Nothing. Say nothing.'

He lifts the Parabellum and stands up, one hand reaching out to grasp my shoulder, and says, 'It does no good, sergeant, to know your enemy.'

'No,' I say, looking after him as he walks down to the water, 'it does no good to know your enemy.'

Seven

It was the sergeant who discovered that the boy had gone. He sat awake during the night looking blankly at the sky, sometimes going down to the water's edge, where the dull surface of the lough failed also to arouse his mind. The man too was restless and the sergeant listened to him moving about. Once he saw him, the man's bulk merging with the night as he stood gazing westward to Donegal and the Atlantic. The two figures were a dozen yards from each other and each wrapped in his own isolation.

It was long after daylight before he finally fell asleep and early evening before he was awake again. He had slept badly. His mouth was sour and his eyelids heavy. And his mind was still dead, as though he had involuntarily blotted out the past week from memory. The man was sitting opposite him, his back against a tree stump, eyes closed, the Parabellum in his lap.

Standing up, it was the unaccustomed weight of the revolver in his pocket which suddenly made him pause. Taking the gun out, he opened it and saw the empty chamber. And then he remembered.

Kneeling on a low bank he splashed the icy water against his face until it burned. His other pocket was heavy too, and from it he took the watch. Clicking open the front he saw that it was well after eight o'clock. Both items were comforting. More, they clothed a nakedness in his being. He was almost that man who walked down the hill to Ballygally with his son at his side. He could see them both clearly.

Coming back he stood in the darkness some way off and watched the man. The latter hadn't moved. Across the lough behind him banks of mist, some thick, some thin, some in human and animal shapes, drifted across the landscape. His gaze returning to the figure at the stump, the sergeant noticed that there was no sign of the rifle. Probably the man had decided to wait until the last moment before taking the .303 so as not to make the boy suspicious. But it was the rifle which was uppermost in the sergeant's mind. Climbing up over the bank where he knew the boy had made a bed, he found the small hollow to be empty. The police greatcoat which the boy had worn throughout the trek was rolled up and tucked among some stones. The grass had been brushed as if to lessen signs of human presence to the casual eye. It was a signal of departure.

Prodding the sleeping figure with his foot the sergeant felt both anger and fear. 'The boy,' he said. 'The boy's gone.'

The man's eyes were open though otherwise he hadn't moved. 'And the rifle?'

'Gone too.'

The man slowly stood up. 'To be fooled by a boy.'

'Fooled? What have we done to him?' There was anger in the sergeant's voice, an increasing anger he wanted to show, and he gripped the man by the arm. 'He must have heard us. And he knows us. Knows us both.'

'I was out today,' the man said, 'for a last look. The border's thick with troops.' Releasing himself from the other's grip, he added, 'But it should be all right to cross.'

'I'm coming with you,' the sergeant said.

'I'll not stop you. We should be able to catch him up. He'll have to go slow because he doesn't know where he's going. Or what he's likely to meet.'

They found the boat untouched. 'At least he didn't take this,' the sergeant said, and as he looked into the other's face saw that he was smiling.

'He'll have no difficulty in the water, the boy. You know, he saved me from drowning. When we escaped.'

In places the mist was thick where they couldn't even see one

153

another though they were only paces apart, and sometimes there were large clear areas closed in by a wall of greyish white in which everything was blindingly clear, as though it were day. When they stumbled into these they would fall and shield their eyes, the man grasping the machine-pistol tightly against his body and the sergeant holding up the empty revolver.

'Ammunition,' he said. 'I want ammunition.'

'For what?'

'Whoever we might meet's hardly going to ask who I am first. Not in this. And an empty gun doesn't give me a chance.'

And because the war didn't matter any more, he thought. There were too many sides and sides he now no longer understood, not even his own. There was only the boy, whose face looked out at him with a different face from every patch of mist.

The man tossed a handful of bullets on the grass. 'Just don't fall behind me.'

'Still don't trust me, eh?' the sergeant said, filling the chamber of the revolver and pushing the remainder of the bullets into his pocket.

'You still might get your wish,' the man said.

'I might that,' answered the sergeant, knowing that he didn't want it.

They were hurrying now, running, taking risks. Once they broke through the mist and found their path barred by a large company of British soldiers. Lights shone behind them which seemed to be a town. Belleek, the sergeant said, and saw the man nod in agreement. Retreating, they moved north then west then curved back south-east again. The boy must be somewhere in this direction, the man said, leaving the sergeant to wonder why he too no longer seemed to care for himself. Lost, they turned again, again, crouching, listening, hearing shouting in the distance, singing, until the lights were in front of them as before and this time there were no soldiers blocking their way.

'Belleek again,' the sergeant said.

'Quiet,' the man said, crouching, ears intent. 'Listen.'

Through the silent air came a dull roaring sound. It rose and fell, at times faded altogether, and sometimes drifted with the breeze that shredded the mist in a tintinnabulation of drums and pipes.

'What is it?' the sergeant asked.

'The Falls. Assaroe Falls. Ballyshannon. We're over the border.'

'Where the hell is the bloody border?' the sergeant shouted.

It was then that they heard the rifle. First there was a single shot, then two in quick succession. Running, bending double, they went up the slope hearing the answering fire coming in two different directions. The mist enclosed them again and still they ran, stumbling, falling, trying, in the lull that followed, to guess accurately the spot from where the rifle had sounded. The gunfire started again, heavier this time, and they broke through the mist in time to see the boy spin violently, the rifle hurtling from his grasp. The sergeant fell to his knees as the man ran on into the mist again. The boy's eyes were open and his right forefinger was pointing upwards and on the shadows across his face he was smiling.

'I see it,' the sergeant said. 'I see it.' Through the mist and the broken cloud a dolphin swam among the stars. 'I see it. It's a dolphin, isn't it? And it's free.' It was then the sergeant realised that the boy's right hand was held up by a tree root and the eyes that glistened to the night sky were dead.

The rattle of the machine-pistol was relentless. When it stopped he heard the pistol firing. Shooting was coming from both sides of them now. Standing up, the sergeant held the revolver out and began following the man through the mist as all fell silent again.

'Who are you?'

The group of soldiers stood in his way, their guns aiming at him.

'Sergeant Duncan McKinzie, Royal Ulster Constabulary.'

'And who are they?'

'Soldiers of the Republic.'

'This is the Free State.'

Another voice joined in, shouting from some distance behind them, an English voice.

'Who were they?'

'Republicans,' the Free State officer shouted. 'Republicans. We both got them.'

'I was their hostage,' the sergeant said.

'You can go back now,' the officer said. 'We want no trouble with you. You're free.'

'I was their hostage,' the sergeant repeated. 'They escaped from a prison-ship. And came here to fight for the Republic.'

'There is no Republic,' the officer said. 'This is the Free State. You're no one's hostage now. Go back. And a Happy New Year.'

'You're wrong,' the sergeant said. 'I'm still a hostage. No. Not yours. Now I'm a hostage of the dead.'

'Go back.'

'Where is this place?' the sergeant asked.

'Ballyshannon.'

'That's where they were going. That's where I was going. I'll take them the rest of the way.'

Going to where the boy lay he grasped him by the heels and dragged him to the body of the man. The man lay on his side, the Parabellum beside him, the pistol still in his hand, a line of bullet holes running across his chest at an angle. Slipping off the belt from his greatcoat the sergeant tied it round the feet of both and, looping his right arm in the sling, began to drag them on.

He went down the slope to Ballyshannon, talking, laughing, crying, his finger pointing to the sky, the Free State soldiers looking at him, wondering, as he dragged his dead, heads cracking on stones, past the majesty of the Falls and the winking beaming eye of Paddy's Lighthouse and the huge dome of Paddy's Milestone, to Ballyshannon, a stumbling demented bear, to where the island of legend, Inis Saimer, faces westward brooding on the vastness of the Atlantic and all the beasts of the sea.